The Emerald
Book of Stories

The Emerald
Book of Stories

THE HEAVEN ENCOUNTERS
The Odyssey Begins

Ruby Klein

Illustrated by: Tracey Taylor Arvidson

XULON PRESS

Xulon Press
2301 Lucien Way #415
Maitland, FL 32751
407.339.4217
www.xulonpress.com

© 2020 by Ruby Klein
Illustrated by: Tracey Taylor Arvidson

Printed in the United States of America.

ISBN-13: 978-1-6305-0769-5
Ebook: 978-1-6305-0770-1

Dedicated to the Messenger who visited me and brought the inspiration I needed to start the journey

In addition, my family and friends who encouraged me along the way.

MATTHEW 22:37-40

Jesus said unto him, Thou shalt love the Lord thy God with all thy heart, and with all thy soul, and with all thy mind. This is the first and great commandment. And the second is like it, Thou shalt love thy neighbor as thyself. On these two commandments hang all the law and the prophets.

COLOSSIANS 3:2

Think about the things of heaven, not the things of earth.

Forward by Pastor Meredith Zamora
Cornerstone Church Tri-Cities
www.cornerstonetricities.church

I believe there are so many ways to preach the gospel of Jesus Christ.

Some will hear it from a pulpit, others will experience it sitting across a table while sharing a cup of coffee, while still others will pick up a book, and as they read, experience the power of the gospel shared through a story. I truly believe that God still speaks and is so willing to meet us in a way that each person will understand.

We see it in the ministry of Jesus. He talked to the people in parables and shared stories such as the Shepherd who lost a sheep, the woman who lost a coin, and the father who lost a son. Jesus spoke to people in context that they would understand and relate too.

This book is a beautiful story of purpose and destiny. As you follow Jazelyn's story of discovery, you will find yourself pulled into the pages of this book, and as it unfolds, you will realize the supernatural unseen realm becomes very natural. Ruby has done a great job unfolding the message of salvation, water baptism, and what it means to be a follower of Christ. I believe you will be encouraged as you read this story. Pastors Joey & Meredith Zamora Cornerstone Church Tricities.

Table of Contents

Chapter 1

The Legacy Begins

ONCE UPON A TIME...

Of course, that's the way it always starts...

It was in the days of ordinary disappointments. There was a little girl who lived on the poor side of town. She only had a few friends and was almost invisible to the world; even so, she had a very special heart. She had a heart that could find something good in almost any situation, even in the darkest of times. She was beautiful in her own right. Her name was Jazelyn. She had long, dark lashes that framed her beautiful, large, forget-me-not brown eyes, dark as the night, deep and mysterious, with wild and free-like-the-wind long brown hair that cascaded down her back like a waterfall. She came from a hard-working family and spent many days alone except for her friend Derice, who would show up after her parents left for work. The girls were best friends. They would spend hours and hours on end together.

In those days, the world was covered with sin and darkness, just like today's world. Of course, the sun would shine every day, but there were people hurting each other and telling lies about each other and just for fun stealing from each other. People would do very bad things, and the reason why was because of the dark fog that would float and fly through the skies and hover over people and animals and fill their minds with darkness, sadness and pain, and wickedness. Even with all of the hurt and heartache continually going on, the world trudged forward every day, somehow ignoring and sometimes oblivious to the victims that sin left to die in its wake.

It was summer break for the kids. They had just finished the ninth grade. On a very ordinary morning, Jazelyn's parents left for work and told her that she must wash the dishes and sweep the floor before she could go anywhere or do anything with her friend. "Just another boring day," she thought to herself. "Even worse, another boring summer to endure." However, little did she know that the summer that was unfolding before her would be the most amazing, most important year of her life so far!

She curled up on the couch for a few moments of complete peace and quiet before she started the chores. That is when her life changed. It all started when she murmured a quiet prayer. "God help me!"

Suddenly a voice came from behind her. "Jazelyn, get ready for divine encounters—divine encounters that will cause divine revelation. As you seek My face and behold My glory, I will come to you. It is within Me that you live and move and have your being. Your times are in My hand. I have not left you as an orphan. You have asked for Me to show you My glory, and so it shall be for you and I are one. My Spirit lives in your heart. No one has ever encountered Me without being radically changed. No encounter will ever leave you lacking for those who enter beyond the veil will find a new and living way. In My presence is fullness of joy. As you seek me first, all of the things that you need and desire will be added unto you. The time that we spend together will strengthen you and lift you up and will melt all those cares away. Fix your eyes on Me, Jazelyn, for I Am the Author and Perfecter of your faith. I Am He who was and is and is to come. Look into My eyes, and you will see eternity, deliverance, healing, and blessings forevermore. You will come to know me, and nothing shall be able to sway you. The time has come that you shall know your God and be strong and do exploits, divine encounters for divine revelation. I will rebuke the devourer for you and restore the years that were stolen from you. I am turning things around. These are the times and seasons which the prophets and the righteous ones have longed to see. Watch and see how I pour out My Spirit on all flesh."

Jazelyn jumped up from the couch and turned around quickly, hoping to see who was talking to her, but no one was there. "I must have dozed off," she thought to herself. Just another day that was expected to go along as usual had definitely taken a turn.

Sunlight shone throughout the house, giving it a golden glow of sunrays. A chorus of singing birds broke through the doldrums of the city's hustle and bustle. The air was filled with the comforting aroma of coffee brewing. Through the windows, you could see what seemed to be a million small daisy flowers popping up like buttons in the grass. Jazelyn smiled as she remembered her Grandma always telling her the meanings of flowers. The daisy means innocence and purity. Her favorites were the ones bejeweled by dew in the early morning. They reminded her of tiny ballerinas in their white dresses kissed with rosy pink-tipped edges, dancing over the seas of green lawns with their tenacious spirits.

Jazelyn felt the weight of destiny and the immense burdens of her own expectations. There was an excitement in the air that built as a new dawn arised in her heart, and she felt a readiness inside herself that she had never felt before to begin walking out the story of her life. "It's time; I feel a fire within me, a passion that went from a spark to a bonfire in my soul" she thought to herself. "I feel it deeply inside of me! The energy to give this internal flame to others and watch them become brighter, the fire of the Father that heals others. But what? Where? When?" Only time could reveal the mysteries that were calling her as a whispering wind over a sun-kissed garden.

About halfway through washing the dishes by hand and disinfecting everything she could reach, she noticed a knock on the window. "Hey, come on," said her friend Derice. "It's about time to go hang out at the park." She bounded through the door and leaned lightly against the wall. Her eyes were like an indigo ocean, with pools of iridescent blue, sculpted upon her face like dazzling jewels.

"You have to wait until I get my chores finished," said Jazelyn as she kept up her steady pace of polishing and wiping down everything in sight.

"Fine," said Derice, "I'll just wait for you here on the couch." She dragged her feet over to plop down on the well-worn couch.

"That's fine," said Jazelyn, "but you know we'll get out of here a lot faster if you help me."

"Why do you even care about what the house looks like?" asked Derice. "And why are you such a Miss Goody-two-shoes?" she said, stroking her fingers over the freshly-polished end table.

"Look, it's not that I care about how the house looks, and I'm certainly not trying to be a Miss Goody-two-shoes, but I do love my parents, and they work very hard, and when my parents are happy, I am happy. My grandma always called it respect," grumbled Jazelyn as she kept polishing.

"Okay, fine," said Derice, "I'll help you, but let's hurry up. We're missing out on fun." They hurried to get everything done, and then they headed down the street to the park.

Jazelyn looked around and saw a man yelling obscenities at a small boy. The child was scared, confused and cringing in fear of the enraged man. "Look at that," she said. "Have you ever wanted to change the world and make it a better place?" snapped Jazelyn, kicking some pebbles down the scorched sidewalk.

"Sure," said Derice, "but we're just kids," she remarked, running her fingers down the chain-link fence that they were passing by. "But we can't change the world—we can't change anything! Sometimes I wonder about you and your crazy thoughts," Derice said as she slightly grinned.

"Those are not crazy thoughts!" demanded Jazelyn. "I've seen crazy in some of our relatives, and I can't hold a candle to them. I just have a feeling down deep inside of me that keeps telling me I have to change the world! I don't know how or why or when; all I know is that it's deep inside my soul. It's a small voice telling me to make a difference in some way and change the world," Jazelyn moaned with desperation in her voice. Her thoughts ran rampant in her mind. "How could she talk to me like that? Doesn't she know how much she upsets me when she says hurtful stuff like that?" she thought. Under her breath, she mumbled, "Okay, Lord, I forgive her. Apparently, she doesn't know what she's doing."

"Whatever," said Derice," but I still think you're nuts, but maybe that's why I like to hang out with you. There's never a dull moment." She put her arm on Jazelyn's shoulder, and they both started giggling.

"You do know that there's days when I think you're nuts too, right?" remarked Jazelyn.

Derice grinned, "Well, I only act like I'm nuts so that you don't feel alone in the world. After all, what are friends for?" They both laughed, and all was forgiven.

Now just down the street on the right side of the road lived an elderly woman named Mrs. Joyce. It seemed like whenever they passed by, Mrs. Joyce was out tending her roses and other flowers in her front yard. The house had been made with love, that's for sure. At the height of its glory, it was the jewel of the neighborhood. Down through the harshness of time, its grandeur endured.

Ivy and ferns grew through the crevices of an old winding stone path that led to the back garden. There stood a delicate marble fountain. The soft gurgling of the clear water was melodic as it resonated in the surrounding silence.

Everything there was full of fascination. The old stone cottage was hidden in plain sight, tucked neatly away in a very ordinary urban neighborhood.

Her flowerbeds were like rainbow freckles that adorned her yard like a garland of the most vibrant blossoms softer than any silk. They brought the colors that dreams are woven from. White daisies, lavender, dahlias, roses, the list could go on and on. She had a small house and a fenced-in yard around it, but she had the most magnificent looking gardens. In the backyard, bird songs would drift on the breeze as summertime pollen, as sounds of an enchanted flute, and as soulful as love's first kiss.

"Hello girls," said Mrs. Joyce," what do you have planned for your summer vacation?" as she turned and bent down to pull some weeds. Her aging skin was a soft golden brown, droplets of sweat beaded up on her forehead beneath the brim of her large gardening hat.

"Hi Mrs. Joyce, we don't have much planned this summer. We're just headed down to the park to check and see if any of our school friends are down there," said Jazelyn, stopping to survey the beautiful flowers that filled the yard with a rainbow of color.

Derice nudged her. "Why do you always talk to her? I'm pretty sure she's old and crazy."

"Stop being rude!" said Jazelyn. "Mrs. Joyce makes the best cookies in town."

Mrs. Joyce stood up and turned around and asked, "Do you need any flowers today girls?"

Jazelyn smiled from ear to ear and said, "Oh yes, please. I would love some on my way home from the park. My mom loves your flowers, and they brighten up our kitchen table so much!"

"That's great!" said Mrs. Joyce. "So if you girls stop by on your way home from the park, we can pick a few for your table," Miss Joyce smiled. "How about you Miss Derice? How about some flowers for your mom?"

"Well, I don't have any money, and my mom doesn't really need any flowers anyway," said Derice, fidgeting about, hoping that Mrs. Joyce had not heard her remarks earlier.

"Oh, my flowers aren't for sale," said Mrs. Joyce. "They are only given as gifts! Would your mom like a gift of flowers?"

"Yes, ma'am, that would be very nice, thank you." Derice shyly smiled, but her eyes shined as an uncommon joy twinkled in them. She was not used to adults being polite to kids and giving away flowers for free!

"Awesome," said Mrs. Joyce. "My flowers would be honored to grace your mother's table. Now how about a cookie? I have just made a fresh batch, and they're cooling in the kitchen," said Mrs. Joyce.

"Yes, please," sayid Jazelyn. "You make the best cookies in town!" She paused for a moment. "And by the way, can I ask you a few questions?"

"Sure, anytime!" remarked Mrs. Joyce. She had a look on her face that seemed to say, "I already know what the question's all about."

Derice looked at Jazelyn in surprise. "Are you sure the cookies are not poison?"

"Calm down, Derice! My mother has been friends with Mrs. Joyce for years, and we have had many of her cookies. And since I'm not dead yet, I would say they are not poisonous, and she's not crazy either," replied Jazelyn.

"In fact," smiled Mrs. Joyce, "you girls can help me bake some cookies if you have time and take some home to your families if you would like."

"Awesome," Jazelyn grinned from ear to ear. "That would be great!"

Derice could see how important it was to her friend, so she agreed to bake some cookies and save the adventures at the park for another day. Although she would miss the warm breezes and freshly cut grass with the occasional wild flowers popping up here and there, the friendship they had meant so much more than even the very best day at any park.

A Very Unexpected Encounter

The girls went into Mrs. Joyce's house to bake cookies. "Come on in, girls," said Mrs. Joyce. "The first step to be making excellent cookies is a clean pair of hands. The bathroom is right down the hall, so go wash your hands and be sure to use warm water and soap!"

As the girls walked down the hall to wash their hands, they passed a very large living room, and in that living room was a coffee table that had a huge leather book on it. "Look at the size of this room," said Jazelyn. "It's way too big for this house," trying to figure out how this could possibly be. It looked as large as a conference room. Gold framed pictures of beautiful country landscapes adorned the walls, and a huge floral tapestry rug graced the original handcrafted wooden floor.

"I didn't know this house had such a big room!" said Derice, puzzled as well.

"You're so right!" said Jazelyn. "I've walked around the outside of this house at least a hundred times, and I know that this room is way too large to be in the small house. Okay, I must admit that this is very strange!" said Jazelyn.

About that time, Derice was opening the large book. "What are you doing?" said Jazelyn. "That's private; don't get into other people's stuff!"

"It's fine," said Derice, "it's a coffee table book. People are supposed to look at coffee table books." She opened the book. In the blink of an eye, the large living room became a gymnasium, and it was huge! The girls slammed the book shut and jumped back! "Wow, did you see that?" asked Derice.

"Wowza! Yes, I did—let's get out of here fast!" said Jazelyn. "Let's get back to the kitchen before you get us in trouble."

"No way," said Derice, "I'm going to get to the bottom of this," and ran back to the book. On the front of the book was written in large scrolling letters "The Secrets of the Ages." And under it was inscribed, "Basic Instructions Before Leaving Earth." Derice slowly opened the book. In an instant, the large living room became a huge gymnasium once again. The whole room glowed; the walls glimmered and beamed as if they had diamonds embedded in them. At once, light began to fill the room with angels from heaven and heavenly creatures who were dressed in brilliantly white robes that looked as if they were on fire. They wore glistening golden belts and silver flashing swords that hung from them. They burned with intensity as flames of fire seemed to jump and dance on them. They carried on their backs shimmering, silky, almost transparent wings that rose to meet above their heads, gently fanning a spiritual wind. They rushed and hurried around the girls as if they were not even there.

Now in the back of the gymnasium, it was like a hospital-type place where there were angels who looked as if they were injured; however, they appeared to heal supernaturally fast. Over in the other corner was a place that seemed like a cafeteria where angels and heavenly creatures were sitting around tables praying, eating, and visiting. However, the strangest thing ever was on the east wall; on the east wall were huge airplane hangar doors that were open wide, and there were armies of angels flying in and out of the doors and paramedic angels flying in with the wounded angels. There were angels on crutches and angels who had been hurt in battle and angels with big scars across them, but again, they healed very quickly. The girls stood there frozen in time in amazement. Then one of the heavenly creatures spoke to them, "Make no mistake, the wounded ones have been hurt, rejected, and wounded by the humans who they were sent to guard and protect." Then it walked away with sorrow in its eyes.

Again, Jazelyn heard a voice from behind her. "Come forth, warriors of the tribe of Judah. The Spirit is calling forth My end time warriors. It is the sound of praise and worship that they march to. Victory has been spoken forth into the winds of the Spirit. The four winds from the four corners of the earth are moving! No longer are you following the trail of tears, but you have been translated from darkness into light. The winds of the Spirit are the heavenly path you walk on now. You are not of the earth but of My heavenly kingdom. My garments of salvation and robe of righteousness are your warring garments. The enemy is trembling and quaking as you come forth. My presence in you and My gentleness make you great. The enemy cannot understand this. You are the end time army of praise and fire. You are the army of the tribe of Judah, which fights from a place of rest and great power—fire-power. I have trained your hands for battle; your arms can bend a bow of bronze. I am your shield, and My right hand upholds you. My gentleness will exalt you and lift you up high above every principality and power. I broaden the path beneath you so that your feet do not slip. I gird you with strength. Pursue your enemy for I delight in you! By My Spirit, you shall overtake them; they shall fall under your feet, and you shall recover all!"

Jazelyn whipped around quickly again to find nothing. "Did you see who was talking behind me?"

"There wasn't anyone behind you, silly," commented Derice.

Just then, Mrs. Joyce called from the kitchen, "Are you girls ready yet? We need to get this cookie show on the road if you ever want a warm cookie." The girls closed the book, and all was still and quiet in the large living room. They rushed to get their hands washed and back to the kitchen.

"Wonderful," said Mrs. Joyce. "I smell lots of nice rose and lavender soap and water."

The girls did not want to tell her about what they had experienced in her living room and that in the bathroom, they had spilled the soap all over themselves trying to hurry. No one could miss the distinct aroma of rose and lavender that wafted throughout the entire house, making it smell just like Mrs. Joyce's garden.

"I made some lemonade so that we can enjoy it while the cookies are baking," said Mrs. Joyce. "How about we enjoy it out on the back porch as soon as we get this batch in the oven?"

"Sure," said the girls, so they put some baking aprons on, and before you know it, they were sitting on the back porch with lemonade in their hands.

"Mrs. Joyce," said Derice, "when we went to wash our hands, we saw a very large leather book on the table that has 'The Secret of the Ages' written on the front of it. Can you please tell us what it is?"

"Oh, good," said Mrs. Joyce. "You have discovered my mission!"

"What mission?" asked the girls.

"Well, I am a keeper of The Secrets of the Ages Book," said Mrs. Joyce. "It's a very blessed and special book. And all of the keepers are blessed too; I'm not the only one."

"What do you have to do to be a keeper?" asked Jazelyn.

"Yes, I want to know too!" said Derice.

"It's not easy, but it's worth it," said Mrs. Joyce. "Are you sure you want to know? You'll have a lot to learn, and you'll have to take an oath that will be with you all the days of your life, and you have to share the stories with others."

The girls looked at each other and without hesitation, they both screamed, "Yes! Yes, please teach us, Mrs. Joyce!"

"Okay, but it might be scary at times, and you'll see things that are out of this world, and most importantly, if you don't share The Secrets of the Ages Book with others, the ink will fade off the pages, and the stories in the book and all the information and instructions on how to live and prosper in this world will be lost and gone forever as it fades away."

"No!" screeched Derice "That's terrible. We can't let that happen!" Of course, the girls were filled with curiosity and could not wait to learn more about what was going on in the living room inside the book.

Mrs. Joyce looked at the girls and then looked over at the large trunk out on the porch. "You see that old trunk over there?" she said. "Go and open it up and look inside." The girls nearly fell over themselves to get to the trunk; they couldn't wait to see what was inside of it. They wanted to see if it was anything like what was inside the book. They slowly opened the squeaky lid to peek in to see what was inside. What they saw inside was a bunch of costumes. You could see the puzzled looks on their faces, almost of disappointment. However, as the girls closed the lid of the trunk, stood back, and turned to look at Mrs. Joyce, there was a strange, very large man who stood behind her. He had a special glow about him.

"Hello, girls," he said in a deep, soft, friendly voice. "How are you today, Jazelyn and Derice? I understand that you both are interested in becoming keepers of The Secrets of the Ages."

"Yes, sir" they both said, "but we are only girls, and how do you know our names?" both asked, stepping back in case they needed to run.

"That's easy," said the man. "I've known you since before you were born. I have known your parents since before they were born. I have known everyone in the world since the foundation of the world. I know where they live and what their names are and everything about them. There are no secrets in my world."

"Who are you, and what's your name?" the girls both demanded, attempting to look brave and fearless.

"I am the Messenger. I come from the kingdom. The Eternal Creator and Keeper has sent me. I will be a teacher and a helper for you."

Derice thought in her mind, "This is too weird and crazy but totally cool at the same time."

"Yes," said the Messenger, "you're absolutely correct." Her eyes got as big as saucers as she asked, "How did you know what I was thinking?"

"Because the Eternal Creator and Keeper is all-knowing. He is the Alpha and the Omega, the Beginning and the End. He knows all and He sees all and He is everywhere. He knows every thought before you think it. He knows every action before you do it. There is nothing you can do to hide from Him, and there is no place that you can hide from Him. He knows where you are at all times, and He loves you very much. He hears your every whisper, and He listens to the cries of your heart. He is the Father of Lights and every good gift comes from Him," announced the Messenger.

The girls didn't even notice when Mrs. Joyce went back in the kitchen to get the cookies out of the oven. "Are you ready for cookies, girls? They're hot and fresh," said Mrs. Joyce as she brought a large plate of chocolate chip cookies out on the porch. The aromatic fragrance overpowered every other scent in the vicinity.

"How could there be anything more delightful or delicious?" thought Jazelyn.

"Yes, please," they said, and as they turned around, the Messenger was gone. When Mrs. Joyce came out onto the back porch, she also had an old raggedy book under one arm.

"How about a refill on that lemonade?" she asked as she got comfortable in a deeply padded rocking chair.

"Thank you, that would be great, but you missed the man—he was standing behind you. He was big and he glows and then he was talking to us and, and, and..."

"Calm down girls!" said Mrs. Joyce. "He's a dear friend of mine."

"So how long have you known this Messenger?" asked Jazelyn, reaching for a warm chocolate chip cookie.

"Well, I've known him since I was just a child, but He's known me since before time began. He is the Messenger of the Father of Lights. He is also known as the Holy Spirit, the Spirit of the living God, the Spirit of wisdom, and in the Jewish scriptures, He is Ruach Hakodesh, Spirit of YHWH. It literally means 'Spirit of the holy place.' He gives extraordinary spiritual gifts—words of wisdom, words of knowledge, increased faith, gifts of healings, gifts of miracles, prophecy, discernment of spirits, diverse kinds of tongues, interpretation of tongues; and to these are added the gifts of apostles, prophets, teachers, and helps that are connected to the service of the church, such as helping the poor and the sick and leadership abilities, which are connected with pastors. These are gifts given by the Holy Spirit to individuals; their purpose is to build up the entire church. They are described in the New Testament, primarily in 1 Corinthians 12, Romans 12, and Ephesians 4. In 1 Peter 4, it also speaks of the spiritual gifts. They are related to both seemingly "natural" abilities and seemingly "miraculous" abilities empowered by the Holy Spirit. Gifts of healing are supernatural enablements given to a believer to minister various kinds of healings and restoration to individuals through the power of the Holy Spirit. It is one of the signs that follows believers after the laying on of hands and prayer over the sick. These symbolize that believers are channels of divine power and that healing is the work of the Holy Spirit. Healing is also connected with the forgiveness of sins. We are encouraged to pray for the healing of the sick, even if they do not claim possession of the supernatural gift. Gifts of healing operate along with faith. Faith on the part of the one who prays is essential most of the time and many times, faith on the part of the one being prayed for is important as well.

And in Galatians chapter 5, we learn about the fruit of the Holy Spirit. That is the nine attributes of a person or community living in accord with the Holy Spirit. The fruit of the Spirit is love, joy, peace, patience, kindness, goodness, faithfulness, gentleness, and self-control." Mrs. Joyce was in her element as she worked hard to help others understand the mysteries and secrets hidden in the pages of the BIBLE (Basic Instructions Before Leaving Earth). As they enjoyed the cookies and the lemonade, Mrs. Joyce opened the raggedy book and started telling them stories. She started with the stories in the book that she called Genesis that was inside the raggedy book. It looked like a bunch of all chapters, but Mrs. Joyce said that this was a collection of books that had been all put together in one big book. She called it Basic Instructions Before Leaving Earth. She said that it had an Old Testament and the New Testament.

Mrs. Joyce told the girls to search through the big trunk and see if they could find the costumes that would go with the story that she was telling them. Then she began, and the girls started searching through the trunk. And then she started telling the stories. The girls' imaginations were running wild. It was if a great portal had opened up in the garden, and the girls could watch as the stories were being told and they were acted out right in front of their eyes!

"In the beginning, God created the universe and everything in it simply by speaking. And it was called the Word of God. God created the world in seven days and everything in it. (Gen. chapters 1 and 2). 'God formed man from the dust of the earth and breathed into his nostrils the breath of life' (Gen. 2:7). And the woman was crafted with the rib of man, and they were the first two people on the earth. Their names were Adam and Eve, and they lived in a perfect garden. God would visit them in the evening and walk and talk with them, and it was wonderful. Now, there was a tree in the center of the garden, and God had told them that tree was called the tree of the knowledge of good and evil; and He told Adam and Eve that they could eat of every other tree in the garden except of the tree of life in the center of the garden. If they were to eat of that fruit, they would surely die. And God gave Adam and Eve dominion over everything He had created and told them to take authority over it and make it grow and multiply and fill the earth."

Jazelyn said, "I know this story; we've had this story several times in our Sunday school." She was feeling very comfortable now like she did when her grandmother would tell her stories from the Bible.

"Well, that's good for you," said Derice, "but I've never heard about this before." Not having a Christian mentor in her childhood to take her to church or tell her stories, she felt left out and awkward. She was told at a very young age that life was like a pool of sharks. You had to jump in and learn to swim with them or you would be eaten! She had been raised in a world of fear and regrets, just the more reason to hang out with Jazelyn, where everything was different. Jazelyn had taught Derice more about life in general and how to cope with it than anyone in her family was capable of. Jazelyn told Derice that if she had to swim with the sharks, "You better not do it alone! You better have Jesus with you!"

"Don't worry," said Mrs. Joyce. "We are not going to skip any important parts. I used to be a Sunday school teacher for years, and I want to do my best to help you to understand the stories because the pages will fade in The Secrets of the Ages Book if you don't understand. Now let's get back to the story so you can find out what happens. One day as Eve was in the garden, she noticed a serpent in the tree of the knowledge of good and evil. And the serpent tempted her to eat of the fruit of the tree of the knowledge of good and evil. And he lied to her and convinced her to disobey God. She took the fruit and she ate it, and she gave it to her husband Adam; and unfortunately, ultimately, they disobeyed God and that's when sin came into the world. It came to pass that Adam and Eve had two boys. One was named Cain, and the other one was named Abel. Then Cain killed his brother Abel. Sin ran rampant over the earth, and almost all the people of the earth became so evil that God decided to flood the entire planet, saving only one righteous man named Noah and his family in a large ark (or boat) full of animals. God caused it to rain for forty days and forty nights, and it killed everything that was on the earth. And when the ark came to rest and the waters receded, God repopulated the earth through Noah and his family and all the animals that were on the ark. After that, God put a rainbow in the skies as a promise that He would never again be destroyed by a flood. Then after that, God chose a man named Abram, a patriarch of an especially blessed people, later called Israel. After that, we have the story of Abraham's grandson Jacob. Genesis ends with Jacob's son Joseph by a miraculous chain of events ruling in Egypt, setting up the events of the following book of Exodus."

It seemed like the stories went on and on that afternoon, but time went by so quickly no one even noticed until the portal faded away but left the children with a miraculous download of information.

"It's getting late, and we will have to continue more of the stories another day," said Mrs. Joyce. "I think it's time to go to the garden and get some beautiful bouquets of flowers for your moms."

"I guess it is getting late," Jazelyn said. "I guess we'll have to make the park another day." She felt a peace inside herself and much happier than hanging out at the park.

"I totally agree," said Derice. "But this has been much more fun than the park could ever be." Both girls were full of cookies, lemonade, and stories of history, mystery, and wonder.

Chapter 2

Enter the Warriors

$\mathcal{A}$ few days later, the girls rushed over to Mrs. Joyce's house. Derice wanted to race so they could get there faster. "Hurry up, Jazelyn. I can't wait to see what Mrs. Joyce has in store for us today."

"My goodness, slow down a little!" said Jazelyn, already tired from her morning chores that had to done before she could go with her friend.

"I can't, I simply can't," giggled Derice. "I've been thinking about our last visit with Mrs. Joyce constantly. I can't get it out of my mind. Don't you remember what we saw in the living room? I need to go back, and I need to know more and see more and learn more. I can't wait!"

As soon as the girls got to Mrs. Joyce's house, they found a note on the front door: "Girls, if I'm not back when you get here, just come around to the back porch and get some costumes out of the trunk and make up a skit of what you learned about last time—that way I can know how much you have actually learned. I will be back shortly. See you soon, Mrs. Joyce."

Derice, bubbling with excitement, said, "Well, okay then, let's get to it—remember, we're in training to be keepers of The Secrets of the Ages Book!" So the girls rushed around to the back porch, opened the big trunk, and got right to work on their assignment. Meanwhile outside the garden fence, two boys were passing by, and they heard the girls laughing and having fun. They tried to see through the thick overgrown bushes inside the six-foot high chain link fence.

"Can you see anything, Allan?"

"No, Michael, maybe if you lift me up I can," said Allan.

"Why do I always have to lift you up Alan? Why can't you just lift me up first?" Michael demanded.

"Because, Michael, I have to scope out this joint for my brother. Capiche?" snarled Allan. "And don't forget—I'm in charge!"

"Okay, hurry up then because I want to see to!" said Michael. "But when do I get to be in charge?" he said, lifting Allan as high as he could.

"It's no use," said Allan, "I can't see anything. We're going to have to try a different place." He crawled over Michael's back to get down. The boys searched the fence line until they found an opening by the gate.

Jazelyn heard the boys and stormed over to see them. "What are you two troublemakers doing here?" She commanded them to leave immediately, if not sooner!

Allan became very outraged at this and was ready to go fisticuffs with a girl! "What are you girls doing in this yard?" demanded Allan. "I know you two don't live here. You live in the project houses," he said, trying to push her up against the fence.

"So?" snapped Jazelyn. "We were invited to be here by Mrs. Joyce," she said, shoving him backwards as if he were a rag doll. Even though he was taller than her, she was fierce and unstoppable.

"I don't believe you," snarled Allan. "Mrs. Joyce isn't even home. Her car isn't even in the driveway!" He could plainly see that Jazelyn was very strong and had no intentions on letting a boy push her around.

About that time, Mrs. Joyce pulled up, and the girls went running to meet her. "Mrs. Joyce!" said Derice, "we have a major problem here!"

"Oh, dear," said Mrs. Joyce. "What on earth is wrong?" she said as she slowly got out of the car.

Jazelyn was so mad that she could hardly speak. "You see, Mrs. Joyce, these boys are troublemakers to the max!"

Allan piped up, "Well, I oughta…" making a fist at her.

"Leave!" snapped Jazelyn. "Yes, I certainly agree that you two oughtha leave! And right now would be fine. Don't ever come back either!" she said, grabbing his fist and pushing it away.

"Hold on a minute," said Mrs. Joyce. "I think I know how to fix this problem. I have four bags of groceries in the car, so each of you grab a bag and gently carry it into the kitchen for me. And then we will discuss a few things."

The girls looked at each other with amazement. "I can't believe she let those no-good scoundrels stay!" said Jazelyn.

"Me either," said Derice disgustedly, putting her hands on her hips as she stormed over to the car to get a bag of groceries.

"Wait a minute, I just might have a plan," said Jazelyn. "If they get to see what we did, I'm sure it will scare the pants off of them, and they'll run out of here and never come back!"

"Okay, I hope you're right!" said Derice, worried that Jazelyn was going to beat up Allan and then Mrs. Joyce wouldn't let them come over to her house again. After all, she knew how strong-willed Jazelyn was.

When they got back into the kitchen, Mrs. Joyce was busy unpacking her groceries and getting to know the boys.

"I just bought some cupcakes at the market today, so how many of your kids would like a cupcake? I have chocolate and vanilla," said Mrs. Joyce. Of course, everyone wanted a cupcake! "Well, all right then," remarked Mrs. Joyce. "Everyone hurry up and wash up. The girls can show you boys where the bathroom is, and don't forget to use warm water and soap!"

The girls looked at each other and grinned and giggled.

"This is our chance to freak out those hooligans," said Jazelyn.

"Yep, I think this should do it!" commented Derice.

As the kids started down the hallway, Jazelyn grabbed Allan's shirt. "Listen here, creep, we know who you are, and we know where you live," Jazelyn snarled at Allan.

"That goes for you too, punk!" Derice said as she got in Michael's face.

Jazelyn gave Allan the stink eye. "We know that your big brother is in a bad gang, and if anything happens to Mrs. Joyce's home or anything in it or her..."

Allan made a fist. "Well, I oughta..." shaking it at Jazelyn.

"Just consider yourself warned!" she said. "My mom's friend has a son who's a police officer, and I swear I'll tell him everything! By the way, creep—don't you dare go into Mrs. Joyce's living room and open that big leather book on the coffee table. That book is priceless!"

Then the girls stormed off into the bathroom to wash up.

"Did you hear that Michael?" asked Allan. "You stand by the door and keep guard. Just let me know when they are coming—I have to get a good look at that priceless book!"

"I don't know, Allan, maybe this isn't the right time to check it out?" said Michael. "Do you know how mean those girls can be? Last Saint Patty's Day, I pinched Derice, and Jazelyn got in the middle of it and nearly beat the snot out of me!"

"Quit whining about those dames, Michael. I've got to see that book, capiche?" Allan quickly sneaked into Mrs. Joyce's living room and flipped open The Secrets of the Ages Book. In a flash, everything was changed! It scared Allan so bad that he screamed, and he jumped backwards and fell on the floor quivering. Michael was watching from the doorway.

"Oh great," he said, "now you've really done it! We're going to jail for sure now!" Michael was terrified. The girls came running down the hallway. The room was completely gone now. They were standing in the clouds overlooking a great city they didn't even recognize.

"So, Allan, how are you going to explain this?" snarled Jazelyn.

Derice slowly turned around and saw hundreds or maybe even thousands of heavenly beings flying down from the heavens. They were like clear glass, and yet she could see them clearly, but their bodies rippled like the surface of a still pond. Then she looked over, and standing beside Michael was the Messenger. "Oh great," she said, "now we're all in trouble!"

Chapter 3

The mission becomes real.

"Welcome, children!" exclaimed the Messenger with a smile on His face.

"Oh, Mr. Messenger, I'm so sorry!" gasped Jazelyn. "I told Allan to stay out of Mrs. Joyce's living room and not to touch the Secret of the Ages Book. But I see that he didn't listen to me."

"Okay, okay!" piped up Allan in his own defense. "I'll definitely listen to you next time, I promise," he said with his knees shaking like the leaves on a tree in the wind.

"Don't be afraid," said the Messenger. "No one can come to the Father of Lights or see anything concerning Him unless He calls them."

"What are you saying, Mr. Messenger?" asked Jazelyn, watching Him glow again, and she thought she could almost see clear wings.

"Wait a minute, do you know this guy?" Allan said, whipping his head around at Jazelyn, looking at her like she was some kind of Martian or alien.

With His kind and loving voice, the Messenger said, "Don't worry, children; you will know the truth, and the truth will set you free. Look around and tell me what you see."

Michael was so stunned that he could hardly speak. "I see, I see hundreds and maybe even thousands of heavenly beings that are battling the dark fog. And the dark fog changes shapes and sometimes looks like wolves and creatures I've never seen before. It flies, and it slithers around in the darkest places. It appears that the dark fog is stalking people and animals and making them sick and causing them to do bad things to each other. However, the heavenly beings are flying down with huge flaming swords and trying to save as many victims as they can, but some of the people won't let the heavenly beings save or help them at all. I don't understand why they won't let the heavenly beings help them! The people are sick, dying, and suffering and still will not let the heavenly beings help them. This doesn't make any sense to me at all," moaned Michael.

All the kids agreed that they saw the very same thing. The Messenger looked around. "You have seen well, my little friends. And because you have seen well, I can tell you that each one of you has been chosen from the foundation of the world to become the children of the Father of Lights."

"Does that mean we will change the world?" asked Jazelyn.

"In time, you will have the answers that you seek, My child," the Messenger replied.

Derice looked at Jazelyn. "You and that changing the world thing, are you ever going to give it a break?"

"I don't know if I can, Derice. I just don't know if I can," mumbled Jazelyn.

All at once, they were standing in Mrs. Joyce's living room again, and all was still and quiet again. The children just stood there and stared at each other, and Jazelyn said to the boys, "You might as well know that we are in training to be the keepers of this Secret of the Ages Book. Because if no one reads it and learns from it, the writings on the pages will fade away, and it will never be available to mankind ever again. Never, ever again! Do you capiche, Allan?" she said, standing over him like a cat ready to pounce on a mouse.

"Yes, yes, okay, I understand. I want to help too! This book is priceless. You were totally right—it's totally priceless!" exclaimed Allan, still stunned and amazed about the encounter they had just experienced.

"You guys better hurry up and go wash your hands, or Mrs. Joyce will send you back to do it. Don't forget to use warm water and soap!" said Derice. "Don't spill the soap, or the whole house will smell like roses and lavender!" She snickered to herself, "I'm so very thankful to be back and for everything to be okay again."

"Me too," said Jazelyn with a sigh of relief in her voice. "Maybe, I might be a little easier on the boys from now on and not try to trick them, as much—well, maybe... we'll see." A spark of trust was beginning to grow in her heart; however, only time could tell if it could possibly grow into anything lasting.

When everyone got back to the kitchen, Mrs. Joyce asked if everyone had washed up real good. "I don't think you kids were in there long enough to get washed up real good," she said. "Maybe I should do a hand check before you have your cupcakes." All hands stretched out for a cleanliness check. The kids looked at each other.

They had thought for sure they were going to be gone a long time. They had had an encounter that they could not explain or deny. A bond between them that could not be broken had been formed.

Mrs. Joyce told the kids to each grab a cupcake and head out on the porch. She grabbed a glass of lemonade and the raggedy book and said, "I'm right behind you. Everyone pick a place to sit, and let's bless our food. Father, bless our food and all the hands it took to prepare it and the company that we share today. In Jesus's name, amen," she prayed.

"Mrs. Joyce, why do you have such an old raggedy book?" asked Alan as he pointed to the torn and worn-out pages of the book she had brought outside with her.

"Well," she replied, "it's like an old friend to me. It is my Basic Instructions Before Leaving Earth, and I've had it since I was a little girl. Nevertheless, enough about me—let's talk about the pressing issues at hand. Now, it is clearly evident that you girls are upset about the boys being here. So, I have a perfect solution to the problem. Anyone wanting to come back and play in my garden must make a very important decision about his or her life and consider what it means to take the oath of The Secrets of the Ages Book. It's not something that you should take lightly; it's a very blessed and sacred oath that will be with you always and forever. And if you decide to take the sacred oath, your name will be written in the Lamb's Book of Life."

"Sign me up right now," said Allan.

"Me too," said Michael.

"Hold on a minute!" said Mrs. Joyce. "I haven't even told you anything about it yet. Do you even know what sacred means? It means sanctified, holy, and set apart for God, the Father of Lights, the Creator and Keeper of life. Do you remember the Christmas nativity story, where the baby Jesus is born in a stable and laying in a manger?"

"Sure we do," said the kids.

"Good," said Mrs. Joyce, "then we need to talk about the prayer of salvation, which is the sacred oath that I'm talking about.

How to have Eternal life

#1- Believe that you have sinned against God and Jesus can save you. 'All have sinned and fall short of the glory of God' (Rom. 3:23).

#2- Ask Jesus to forgive you and to make your heart clean. 'If we confess our sins, he is faithful and just and will forgive us our sins' (1 John 1:9).

#3- Tell Jesus you want Him to be your Lord and Savior of your life. 'If you declare with your mouth Jesus is Lord and believe in your heart that God raised him from the dead you will be saved' (Rom. 10:9).

#4- Trust Jesus to free you from the habit of sinning and to give you a new life that goes on forever. 'Now that you have been set free from sin, the benefit you reap leads to holiness, and the result is eternal life' (Rom. 6:22).

Now let's talk about this," said Mrs. Joyce. "How many of you have ever told a lie? Or said you didn't do something when you really did? Or did something when you were told not to do it?"

The kids all looked at each other. "Well that means we all have sinned every day!" said Allan, fidgeting in his chair.

"You're very right," said Mrs. Joyce, "so let's put a checkmark on the first item. Now who wants Jesus to forgive them and make their heart clean?"

Everyone said, "I do, I do!"

"Okay, let's put a checkmark on the second item also. Now who remembers the Easter story, when Jesus was hung on the cross and bled and died for our sins? 'God so loved the world that he gave his only son that whoever would believe in him would not perish but have everlasting, eternal life' (John 3:16). The next step is to tell Jesus that you want Him to be your Lord and Savior of your life. 'If you declare with your mouth Jesus is Lord and believe in your heart that God raised him from the dead, you will be saved' (Rom. 10:9)."

The children all agreed that they should put a checkmark in that box also.

"And the last step of the oath is to trust Jesus to free you from the habit of sinning and to give you a new life that will go on forever. 'But now that you have been set free from sin, the benefit you reap leads to holiness and the result is eternal life' (Rom. 6:22). Well," said Mrs. Joyce, "who wants to trust Jesus to free them from the habit of sinning, and who wants a new life that goes on forever?"

"We do! Yes, we do!" all the kids agreed.

"Okay," said Mrs. Joyce. "Let's see if we can put it all together. Repeat after me," said Mrs. Joyce.

The Prayer of Salvation.

"Our gracious, loving, Heavenly Father, I come to You in the name of Jesus; I admit that I am a sinner. Right now, I choose to turn away from sin and ask You to cleanse me from all unrighteousness. I believe with all my heart that Jesus died on the cross to take away my sins and then He rose from the dead so that my sins would be forgiven and made righteous through faith in Him. I now confess that Jesus is my Savior and Lord and pray that You will fill me with Your power of the Holy Spirit. I declare that I am now saved and set free from sin; I am a child of God, and my name is now written in the Lamb's Book of Life. In Jesus's name, amen.

If you prayed that prayer and meant it, you are now a child of God, the Father of Lights, Keeper and Creator of all things. The Bible has many more life-changing promises for you than you can ever imagine. 'For whosoever shall call upon the name of the Lord shall be saved' (Rom. 10:13). 'Therefore if any man be in Christ, he is a new creature, the old things are passed away, Behold, all things are made new' (2 Cor. 5:17).

When you receive Christ into your heart, you join a special family," said Mrs. Joyce, "the family of God. You begin your life in Jesus Christ. And the journey that you are starting is an exciting one as you discover God's plan for your life and live it out each day, starting today! 'My people are destroyed for lack of knowledge' (Hos. 4:6). Today, plan to start learning more about God and seeking Him daily through Bible study and prayer to unlock your destiny. 'Seek first the kingdom of God and his righteousness, and all these things shall be added to you' (Matt. 6:33). 'If you love me, keep my Commandments' (John 14:15). 'And Jesus said to him you shall love the Lord your God with all your heart and with all your soul and with your entire mind. This is the great and first commandment. And the second is like it, you shall love your neighbor as yourself' (Matt. 22:37-39). 'In everything give thanks, for this is the will of God in Christ Jesus concerning you' (1 Thess. 5:18).

The first step toward doing God's will for your life is to make sure that you have Jesus living in your heart. Goodness will surround you the minute you are in the will of God. You will find goodness everywhere you go. Everything you touch will be blessed. This doesn't mean you won't have challenges—far from it, but you will have the peace in the problems. Praise God! Man is created in the image of God, unique among all creation (Gen. 1:26-27, Eph. 4:24, Col. 3:10). Those who repent of their sins and trust in Jesus Christ come to resemble God the Father in Christ; they are created in God's image. God deals with human beings as creatures made in His image and determines His plan for them before they are born (Gen. 25:23, Jer. 1:4-5, Isa. 49:1-2,5, Gal. 1:15). 'Let him turn to the Lord, and he will have mercy on him, and to our God, for he will freely pardon' (Isa. 55:7). 'I, even I, am He who blots out transgressions, for my own sake, And remembers your sins no more' (Isa.

43:25). 'For I will forgive their wickedness and remember their sins no more' (Jer. 31:34). Jesus is the reason.

'And he said to them, go into all the world and preach and publish openly the good news (of the gospel) To every creature (of the whole human race.) He who believes (who hears and trust in and relies on the gospel and in him who it sets forth) and is baptized will be saved (from the penalty of eternal death, but he who does not believe who does not adhere to and trust and rely in the gospel and him who sets forth) will be condemned' (Mark 16:15-16 AMP). 'All things are from God who through Jesus Christ reconciled us to himself (received us into favor, brought us into harmony with himself) and gave to us the ministry of reconciliation (that by the word and the deed that we might aim to bring others into harmony with him)' (2 Cor. 5:18 AMP).

God wants to bless you. 'Happy is the man who finds wisdom, and the man who gains understanding (Prov. 3:13). 'The Lord blesses the habitation of the just (Prov. 3:33). 'The blessing of the Lord makes us rich and he adds no sorrow with it' (Prov. 10:22). 'Blessed is the one who fears the Lord always, but whoever hardens his heart will fall into calamity' (Prov. 28:14). 'I walk in the way of the righteous, along the powers of justice, bestowing wealth on those who love me and making their treasures full' (Prov. 8:20-21). God is love—be blessed.

Congratulations children," said Mrs. Joyce, "your names are now written in the Lamb's Book of Life. And now, are you ready to receive your armor?" The children looked at her in amazement.

"Armor?" asked Allan and Michael. "What do you mean armor? Yes, of course we want the armor!"

Jazelyn and Derice looked at each other. "Well if the boys get armor, we want some armor too!"

"Okay then," said Mrs. Joyce, "the days are evil, so we need to dress appropriately. Armor—to fortify yourself, to spiritually equip yourself for a battle. Let's read Ephesians 6:10-18. The helmet of salvation—an essential item for soldiers' survival. The helmet protects the head of the soldier, where there is the mind and the spirit. Our salvation comes from Jesus, and it is an everlasting protection until the day we are with Him in heaven. Your mind must be protected with a helmet that's able to absorb the shocks of being hit by the enemy and even knocked to the ground in the spiritual realm. The enemy is trying to stop us from accomplishing the things that God has for us to do. God has a few secrets He wants us to hear. They are secrets because oftentimes, what God has to say to you is meant for you only and no one else.

Satan does not want us to wear the helmet because he wants his whispers to become the false reality through which we interpret and respond to life. Every victory you are ever going to experience has already been won. All of the power you need to live the life that God has created for you to live is already yours.

The breastplate of righteousness—the typical Roman soldier wore a protective covering to cover the vital organs, like the heart, the lungs, liver, etc. If any of these were injured, the life of the soldier would be in serious jeopardy. If we try to do battle over Satan's enemies with only our own righteousness, we will never win. We need a righteousness that comes from our Savior Jesus. The breastplate of righteousness surrounds us with secure protection in warfare we so desperately need. Feed your spirit with the Word of God so that the Spirit will produce the natural outgrowth of right living within you.

The belt of truth—the belt worn by a Roman soldier was important because it firmly secured the soldier's weapon needed to fight. If we are to stand up to evil, we must be firmly secure by the truth that is found in only Jesus.

We need to wear the belt of truth at all times. God has already predetermined truth. When you follow His truth, He will empower you to overcome the lies of the enemy and fight your spiritual battles with spiritual authority.

The shield of faith—the shield protected the Roman soldier from arrows and sword blows. Our spiritual enemies are constantly throwing arrows and thrusting swords toward us. The best way to deflect these blows is with the shield of faith. When we hold onto our shield, then we hold firm to our faith in Jesus; we can go forth boldly. Faith is critical for achieving victory in spiritual warfare. The Scriptures are full of verses that speak about the weapon of faith and where to find it. 'Jesus is the author and perfector of our faith' (Heb. 12:2) 'For whatever is born of God overcomes the world' (1 John 5:4). The key to winning in warfare is faith. Pick up the shield of faith and grab the victory that has already been won.

The sword of the spirit—the Roman sword was short and lightweight so that they could use it easily. At close range, it was a deadly weapon. The sword of the spirit represents the Word of God. The Word of God is a powerful weapon, especially when used under the power and guidance of the Holy Spirit. The sword of the spirit is the only offensive weapon in your arsenal. With it, you can attack and advance—the only one the Spirit uses in the spiritual realm. It is The Word of God. Using the sword of the spirit means communicating to the enemy specific scriptures that relate to your unique situation.

Our feet are covered with the gospel of peace. To do battle, a soldier must be prepared to go, and good strong sandals are absolutely necessary. They give a soldier a sure footing, making mobility in battle easier, while also making it more difficult to be knocked down. The spikes on the bottom of your 'peace shoes' dig down deep into the solid ground beneath you. When your feet are covered with the preparation of the gospel of peace, it creates a stability that Satan cannot undo. God offers us a peace that reaches beyond what we can comprehend. When worry creeps back in, you need to remind yourself that it is lying to you because God has promised that He will always provide for you. Likewise, before we can go do battle, we must be prepared, but our preparation comes from the gospel. The gospel is the good news about Jesus, and through it, we can tell others how they can have peace with God.

Prayer is how you get dressed for warfare. It is how you put on the armor. It is the earthly permission for heavenly interference and intervention. 'Our struggle is not against flesh and blood, but against the rulers, against the powers, against the world forces of darkness, against the spiritual forces of wickedness in the heavenly places' (Eph. 6:12).

To pray is to communicate with God with conversation, thanksgiving, and praise, and it is where the Holy Spirit is heard and where you share your thoughts, intents, concerns, and desires to Father God.

Now," said Mrs. Joyce, "let's discuss a few things. #1- Why do we need spiritual armor?"

Jazelyn piped up, "To stand against the wiles of the evil one."

"Very good," said Mrs. Joyce. "#2- What is it we fight against?"

"Against the rulers, against the authorities, against the power of the darkness in the dark world, and against the spiritual forces of evil and heavenly realms," said Allan.

"That must be the ghosts, goblins, and lost souls that's always flying around the scary movies," chimed in Michael. "My grandpa calls them princes of the air and demons."

"Very good," said Mrs. Joyce. "You have listened well. #3-Should we be afraid of this battle?"

"No, God will help us stand against the evil powers of darkness, and it will be defeated by God," said Michael.

"#4- How does God help us in the battle against evil?"

"He gives us the weapons and armor we need to stand strong," said Michael.

"#5- Why is it important that we put on our spiritual armor every day?" Mrs. Joyce asked as she smiled, knowing that they understood well.

Derice said, "I know, I know! Without it, we will be weak and easily defeated by the enemy."

"Very good," said Mrs. Joyce, "I am very impressed! It is getting late now, so why don't you kids come back next week, and we will bake dog cookies for the Humane Society. They have a special recipe, and it will give us some more study time." Everyone was thrilled—finally, an adult who took the time to teach them about the spiritual world and the things of God in a way that they could understand and who made the experience fun and real. They couldn't wait to get back and learn more. Mrs. Joyce made learning something that was exciting. She had a perfectly simple way of using a little patient observation and a warm dose of love to discover the God-given talents within people. It was easy for her to fill a person with pure happiness, one born of curiosity and the anticipation of discovery of new things.

Later, the boys were walking home and noticed a few of the kids who hung around with Allan's brother. "You know they're up to no good!" Michael grabbed Allan by the shirttail. "Don't let them see you!"

"Don't worry—I don't intend to." The boys stepped back into a large bush to watch from a distance. "I can't understand why those guys thought it would be a good idea to join that creepy gang. They all have good families!" Allan muttered under his breath. "Nobody joins a gang without being a lost soul first. No one goes to a monster for guidance unless they think it is their only option. Gangs steal kids from their family's one piece at a time. Every week they're pushed a little further until not only do they have no morals but their families become their enemies! They forge bonds for selfish gain, masquerading as a brotherhood. All that keeps them fired up and moving is energy from the dark side. My brother and I used to have so much fun together, but now it's like two strangers living in the same house. He has a desire for the joy of power, an addiction to inflicting fear, and a hunger to increase their adrenaline to ever higher heights."

Michael sunk back farther into the large bush. "I have walked these streets my whole life. I used to feel calm and at home here, but not today—my heart wants to beat out of my chest! It is pounding like it's going to crack a rib. Ever since the bikers came to town, marking out their turf like a wolf pack, the gangs started popping up. Let's get out of here before we witness something we'll be sorry for!"

"You're right—they want to dominate everyone, regardless of reason or rhyme," agreed Allan. The boys quietly snuck out and headed to Michael's house until they knew for sure Allan's mom was home from work.

Chapter 4

Every Creature has a Voice

About a week later, Jazelyn was rushing around, trying to get her chores done before going to Mrs. Joyce's house. She was ecstatic, thinking about the supernatural encounters they would have that day. She was singing and dancing, and her heart was filled with so much joy and happiness that she hadn't felt in such a long time, maybe even never before. Suddenly, there standing in the room was the Messenger.

"Hello. Jazelyn," He said. "I need you to pray for Allan."

"But Mr. Messenger, I don't even like Allan, well, very much." Jazelyn tried not to look at the Messenger because her heart was softening toward Allan but she wasn't ready for anyone to discover it yet.

"That's not the point," He said. "I need you to pray for Allan now."

"Okay, okay—Lord please bless Allan, in Jesus's name, amen. There, I did it." But when she turned around, the Messenger was gone. "How strange," she thought to herself.

Not long after that, Derice showed up at the front door. "I had the strangest morning," she said, "I had a visit from the Messenger, and He told me to pray for Allan."

"Oh, really," said Jazelyn. "He came to visit me and told me the same thing."

"Did you do it?" asked Derice.

"Yes," said Jazelyn, "even though I didn't want to—there's only one boy in this whole town who gets on my nerves, and it's Allan. But I remembered Mrs. Joyce telling us that the mirror of a man's heart is his actions and to do unto others as you want them to do unto you. And to love your neighbor as yourself."

"Yeah, I remember her saying that also," said Derice. "It's kind of funny, but as much time as we spend over at Mrs. Joyce's house, it seems like I hear her voice all the time, teaching us things about the mysteries and the knowledge of The Secrets of the Ages Book."

"Yeah, me too," said Jazelyn. "Come on, I've got my chores done. Let's get over to Mrs. Joyce's house. I'm anxious to see what kind of mysteries we will learn about today." On the way to Mrs. Joyce's house, they ran into Michael.

"Where is Allan?" asked Jazelyn.

"I don't know," said Michael. "I haven't heard from him, and I had a visit from the Messenger this morning, telling me to pray for Allan."

"Wow, you're kidding right?" said Derice.

"No, I'm not," said Michael. "It really freaked me out!"

"Okay, said Jazelyn. "Something's got to be up. We need to stop right here, right now, and say a prayer for Allan. I know that he would not miss out on making dog biscuits at Mrs. Joyce's house if something wasn't wrong." The kids stopped and made a circle. "Everyone hold hands," said Jazelyn. "I remember Mrs. Joyce said that a three-strand cord is not easily broken, so I think we need to do it this way."

"I agree," said Michael, "I've seen people in Mrs. Joyce's church pray like this."

Derice looked at Michael. "When did you go to church with Mrs. Joyce?"

"I didn't," said Michael, "but I did go with my grandma and grandpa, and Mrs. Joyce was there."

"Oh, I was just wondering," said Derice. Deep in her heart, she wished she had someone to take her to church. She thought to herself, "Someday, when I have my own kids, I'm definitely taking them to church!"

"I want to say the prayer," said Michael.

"Sure," said Jazelyn, "Go right ahead. I don't like him. He always seems to make me mad, and so I don't know what to pray for him anyway." She turned away slightly so that no one would see her blush.

"Don't you know, Jazelyn?" whispered Michael. "He really likes you. He says that he doesn't. Nevertheless, I can tell that he does." Michael giggled like a schoolgirl.

"I think you're nuts, but whatever—just hurry up and say the prayer. We look weird out here in the middle of the sidewalk holding hands," said Jazelyn.

They all laughed. Michael prayed a magnificent prayer.

"Heavenly Father, we come together to lift up our friend Allan to you—only You Father know his needs. We ask that your Holy Spirit will cover him with energy and Your strength to help him to walk courageously through his trials. Please raise up a hedge of protection around him and work out every detail of his life according to Your perfect will. In the mighty name of Jesus we pray, amen."

Both girls were shocked. "How on earth did you learn to pray like that?" asked Jazelyn.

"No kidding," said Derice. "Wow, you don't say much, but when you do, it's powerful!"

"I just pray like my grandparents pray. They pray about everything!" Michael shyly looked downward and said, "Thanks, you guys—that means a lot to me."

Then they hurried off to Mrs. Joyce's house. When they got there, low and behold, Allan was already there.

"What are you doing here?" asked Michael.

"I just had to get out of my house really early," said Allan.

Silently, he thought to himself, "I wish my brother could see how the people he hangs around with have such an inflated sense of their own importance, a deep need for admiration, and a lack of empathy for others, but behind the masks they wear lies a fragile self-esteem that's vulnerable to the slightest criticism. It is not right, and someday I will find a way to teach other kids about how important it is to stay out of gangs—not only for themselves but for their families also."

The girls looked at him very strangely. Somehow, they could tell that Allan was on his own private mission to save the world.

"Well, my big brother and his thug friends took over my house as soon as my mom left for work. Sometimes, they get mean, and I do not want to be around when it happens. Capiche? And sometimes, the less you know, the healthier you stay, capiche?" mumbled Allan.

Jazelyn could tell that Allan wasn't saying everything. He was embarrassed about the things his brother was doing. He was also scared about what might happen to his family if his brother didn't quit hanging out with the rough kids in that gang. Then, what the other kids told Allan almost brought him to tears. However, he was much too macho to show any tears or emotion, so he choked them back, but they were visible anyway.

"We've been praying for you all morning," said Derice.

"That's right," said Jazelyn.

"Me too!" said Michael. "The Messenger came to each one of us this morning and told us to pray for you."

"Wow!" said Allan. "I guess that explains why I was able to get away."

"What do you mean?" asked Jazelyn.

"Oh, nothing," said Allan. "Never mind."

About that time, Mrs. Joyce drove around the corner and into the driveway. "I guess you kids are ready to start baking some doggie biscuits for The Humane Animal Shelter. Well, you know the drill—everyone grab a grocery bag and gently carry it into the kitchen."

"Yes, ma'am," said Allan. Everyone was not only looking forward to baking the doggie biscuits but getting to see what was waiting inside the Secret of the Ages Book was the most exciting thing ever! The kids could hardly wait to go down the long hallway to wash their hands with warm water and soap and on the way sneak into Mrs. Joyce's living room to experience another encounter with that mysterious book.

About that time, Mrs. Joyce turned around and said to the children with her hands filled with all sorts of cookie cutters and baking supplies, "Go wash up, children. My grandmother always used to tell me that cleanliness was next to godliness. So don't forget to use lots of warm water and soap. And hurry back—these doggie biscuits are not going to bake themselves!"

The kids all hurried to scamper down the hall, and, of course, they had to duck into the living room where the huge book sat on the table. Allan and Jazelyn nearly tripped over each other to get the book first. Michael dashed past them both and flung open the book, and the pages made a mighty, rushing wind. All of a sudden, everything was still and quiet. They were in some sort of garden. There were animals that were talking to each other in English. Everything the animals said, the children could perfectly understand. There was a mama rabbit and her babies and Mrs. Squirrel and her babies up in a tree. They were having the most interesting conversation.

"I just don't know how you do it, Mrs. Bunny," said Mrs. Squirrel. "You are one of the most adored and benevolent creatures in this meadow. You have long, pink ears and powerful hind legs and a black button nose and a cottontail. They give you such a cuddly appearance!" said Mrs. Squirrel. "You make raising kids look so easy. And all I ever do is work, work, work, I can't keep my kids at home. They're running all over the place all the time. I can hardly keep up with them. And it drives me nuts to gather nuts all day and then they devour all of my hard work in one sitting! And here you are, never having a hair out of place and looking like some beauty queen. I'm just saying, girlfriend, I just don't know how you do it."

"Calm down, Mrs. Squirrel," said Mrs. Bunny. "And you crack me up, girl. Here you are jumping around all the time from tree to tree. My goodness, and you can go real fast to gather peanuts and corn and the things it takes to keep your family happy. And sweetie, you are no doubt one of the smartest creatures that live here in the meadow, and you only have young a couple of times a year. And here I am—I feel like I'm expecting babies all the time! And I love your big bushy tail!"

Just then, Mrs. Squirrel noticed the children. "Freeze, Mrs. Bunny," she said. "They're right behind you."

Mrs. Bunny slowly turned around and saw the children and gasped, "Who are you?"

Derice said, "We're just the kids in the neighborhood. My name is Derice, this is Jazelyn, this is Michael, and this is Allan."

"What place is this?" asked Jazelyn, "and why can we understand what you are saying? And why do you live in The Secrets of the Ages Book?"

Mrs. Bunny looked shocked. "I'm sure I don't know what you're talking about. And why have you come to our land?" she asked.

Mrs. Squirrel by this time was all a flutter, and she said, "Are you from the legend?"

"What legend?" said Jazelyn.

"You know the one," said Mrs. Bunny, "the one that our parents and grandparents have taught us about down through the generations—the legend that the children of the Father of Lights will come and grow into a great army and save us all from the darkness and evilness that has come into our world and overtaken it."

"Wait a minute—hold on!" said Jazelyn. "We're just kids who are in training to take care of and be the keepers of The Secret of the Ages Book someday."

"Then it's true," said Mrs. Squirrel, "you're here, you're here! I must spread the word. Hurry—tell the rocks to cry out. The children are here, the children from the legend." And Mrs. Squirrel scampered through the trees quickly to tell of the coming of the children from the legend. Then a humming melody was heard throughout the land.

"What is that humming?" asked Allan.

"That's the rocks crying out the good news that you're finally here! The children of the Father of Lights are finally here!" Mrs. Bunny said

"Wow," said Michael, "I really hope you're not disappointed."

Just then the Messenger appeared. "Are you ready for today's journey?" He asked the kids.

"Yes, Sir!" the kids chimed in together.

"What is this place?" asked Jazelyn.

"We all want to know," said Derice.

"This is the Land of Waiting," said the Messenger. "This is the land where all of creation is waiting on you, the children of man to grow up into your destinies as the children of the Father of Lights, to seek Him with all your hearts and be who you were created to be."

"Mr. Messenger," said Mrs. Bunny, "I was just going to take the children on a mini tour of our land so they might understand the importance of their mission."

"Very good," said the Messenger, "I'll come with you. I'm sure they will have questions."

"You better believe it," said Michael.

"Amen, brother!" said Allan. As they walked through a beautiful meadow, they passed a big, lazy bear sunning himself next to a large tree that had a nice-sized honeycomb in it.

Mrs. Bunny called out, "The children of the Father of Lights are awakening! Hurry, hurry, everyone, and make ready! They're waking up! The legend has come. They're waking up!"

The big, lazy bear rolled over and looked at the children. "Well, I'll be a monkey's uncle—my grandma was right!"

A little farther down the path was an old, gray donkey.

Again, Mrs. Bunny called out the news, "Hurry, Hurry! Everyone, make ready! The children of the Father of Lights are waking up! The legend has come!"

The old, gray donkey just took a deep breath, hung his head down, and said, "They probably won't stay. They'll probably just go home and forget about us. It probably won't last."

The children all laughed. "Don't worry, Mr. Donkey. We'll never forget you!" said Derice.

Soon they reached a river. Again, Mrs. Bunny called out the news, "The legend is real. Hurry, hurry, everyone, and make ready. The children of the Father of Lights are waking up!"

They continued down a path that curved and twisted down to meet a large river. "Oh, this is awesome," said Michael, taking deep breaths and enjoying the wonderful smells of the flora and fauna of the meadow.

"Yeah," said Allan, "man, this is a really cool place!" as he observed all the different plants along the edges of the path. "The plants here seem to be more beautiful than anywhere else I know."

"What's this place called?" asked Jazelyn. Just then, a large beaver wearing a workman's hard hat climbed up the river bank right behind her. "Oh my goodness!" said Jazelyn. "Aren't you a big guy!"

"Well, thank you, missy, yes I am!" said the beaver. "My name is Bob, and I'm the foreman of this fine crew of bridge builders." He turned to observe his crew. "Hey, Sam! That log goes a little bit more to the right!" he called out. "Now, to answer your question, missy, this is the Land of Waiting, and this is the River of Destiny," said Mr. Beaver. Everyone looked at the river.

"What are those bubbles that are floating on top of the river?" said Derice. The river danced with effervescence. It had a glow like the aurora borealis. The rich colors like a translucent mother of pearl covered the bubbles as they floated into the air, and each bubble had a story in it, a moving picture.

"Wow, every bubble has a movie inside of it!" said Allan.

Everyone was amazed.

The Messenger smiled. "Good observation!" He said. "Each one of the bubbles belongs to someone in the world. They are called destiny bubbles."

Mr. Beaver waddled over to a huge stone. "Before I forget, I want to show all of you this special rock." The kids ran over to it. On the top of it was carved: "Holding onto Hope is Brave, Happily Ever After begins HERE."

"What does it mean?" asked Jazelyn.

"That, my little friends, is up to you!" the Messenger exclaimed. "In this land, if you look closely enough, you will find lots of clues to your own destinies. What you do with the clues will determine the destiny of each one of you—what you do, wherever you go, and how you share the information of what you learn here, everything."

Michael looked across the river. It was a most beautiful land—a great high mountain, a holy city clothed in God's glory in all its splendor and radiance. The luster of it resembled a rare and most precious jewel like jasper, shining clear as crystal. It had a massive high wall with twelve large gates. At the gates were stationed twelve angels. And on the gates were written the names of the twelve tribes of the sons of Israel. The wall was built of jasper while the city itself was pure gold, clear and transparent like glass. The foundation stones of the walls were ornamented with all of the precious stones. The first foundation stone was jasper, the second sapphire, the third chalcedony (or white agate), the fourth emerald, the fifth onyx, the sixth sardius, the seventh chrysolite, the eighth beryl, the ninth topaz, the tenth chrysoprase, the eleventh jacinth, the twelfth amethyst. And the twelve gates were twelve pearls, each separate gate being built of one solid pearl. And the main street of the city was made of pure gold and translucent as glass (Rev. 21:12). Then, he looked down the river and across. It looked like a scary nightmare. "What are those two lands called?" he asked as he stared at an ancient slumbering forest that had been turned into stone. Lulled into oblivion stood a land long since burned to ash in a sea of pain and flames. The mist vailed the river before it; the shores looked storm-swept with ice and wind that had been twisted with truth and lies. If you looked closer, you could see shapeshifters and wolf-riders circling the land as evil guards.

"Well, the beautiful land straight across is the Land of Eternity. It's where the throne room of the Father of Lights is. And the land down there is the Land of Lost Souls—that's a terrible place. Almost everyone that either goes there or who is captured by the dark fog and taken there never returns," Mr. Beaver said with a frightened tone in his voice. "I don't know who built the bridge over to that land, but it wasn't my crew. We had nothing to do with that bridge. That's a very bad land—it's filled with the dark fog and lots and lots of evil things hiding in there," said Mr. Beaver. "Very rarely has anyone who has crossed over ever been able to make it back."

"How dreadfully terrible!" said Jazelyn.

"No kidding," said Derice.

Allan piped up, "Why don't you just tear down that bridge?"

"No one can get close enough to it because of the wars," said Mr. Beaver.

"What wars?" asked Allan.

"The everlasting wars! You know, the wars over good and evil!" said Mr. Beaver, quivering with fear.

"No, I don't know," said Allan.

The Messenger gently put His hand on Allan's shoulder. "Do you want to know the secrets and mysteries of the Forest of Lost Souls?"

"Definitely!" exclaimed Allan.

"This is the story of Lucifer (Ezek. 28, Isa. 14)," said the Messenger. "The Father of Lights created him. He created him to be the light-bringer and day-star, son of the morning! He was in Eden, the garden of God. Every precious stone was his covering, the carnelian, topaz, jasper, chrysolite, and the emerald; and his settings and sockets and engravings were wrought in gold. He was the anointed cherub that covered with overshadowing wings. He was upon the holy mountain of God. He walked up and down in the midst of the stones of fire like the paved work of gleaming sapphire stone upon which the God of Israel walked on Mount Sinai. He was created blameless in his ways until iniquity and guilt; unrighteousness and evil were found in him. Through the abundance of his commerce, he was internally filled with lawlessness and violence. God then cast him out from the mountain of God as a profane and unholy thing saying, 'I have destroyed you, O covering cherub, from the midst of the stones of fire. Your heart was proud and arrogant because of your beauty; you destroyed your wisdom for the sake of your spender. I cast you to the ground; I lay you before kings, that they might look at you. You profaned your sanctuaries by the great quantities of your sins and the enormity of your guilt, by the unrighteousness of your trade. Therefore I have brought forth a fire from your midst; it has consumed you, and I have reduced you to ashes on the earth in the sight of all who look at you. All the peoples and nations who knew you are appalled at you; you have come to a horrible and terrifying end and you will forever cease to be,' declares the Lord God Almighty."

Ezekiel 28:16-19

Mrs. Bunny got a very puzzled look on her face. "I thought you were in training to be keepers of The Secrets of the Ages Book?" she said.

"Yes, we are, but we just started training a few weeks ago," said Jazelyn.

"Oh, great," said Mrs. Bunny. "Now everyone will be brokenhearted if they have to wait another thousand years for the legend to become real." Mr. Beaver gasped and hung his head.

"Well, even if we're not from your legend, we'll still do what we can to help you. Right, everyone?" said Michael.

"Yes, for sure!" agreed Allan. "My family has always said that there was no such thing as good or evil or the supernatural world, but I've seen it with my own eyes!" Today he had seen the truth, and the truth had set him free.

"That's right!" exclaimed Jazelyn.

"Everytime I tell my family about the things I've seen, they think I'm crazy," babbled Derice. "But that's not going to stop me from helping you too." Her spiritual eyes had also been opened, and now nothing could stop her from believing in the sacred mission!

"Wonderful, then maybe you would like to see more of the tour of our land?" asked Mrs. Bunny. Unanimously, the kids all agreed to continue the tour.

Mr. Beaver glanced over at his work zone. "I have to get back to work, but if you want to see a real bridge then just stick to this trail. And don't forget to look for message rocks along the way," he said as he climbed back down the river bank and joined his crew.

They had only gotten a little way down the trail when the Messenger stopped and stood still. Michael was the first one to notice. "Stop, you guys," he said.

Everyone turned around and hurried back to see why the Messenger was stopped. "Children, read this," He said. Again, on top of a big rock, something else was carved.

Allan read it to everyone. "For we are not contending against flesh and blood, but against the principalities, against the powers, against the world rulers of this present darkness, against the spiritual hosts of wickedness in the heavenly places" (Eph. 6:12).

"I know that verse!" said Jazelyn. "Mrs. Joyce has told us that verse many times."

"That's right!" said Derice. "It's from The Secrets of the Ages Book."

"Yes, it is," said the Messenger. "Do you remember what you saw from the top of the mountain the last time you visited The Secrets of the Ages Book?—the city and all of the heavenly creatures battling?" He asked.

"Man, I'll never forget that," said Allan.

"Me either," said Michael. Everyone agreed that they were never going to forget that experience.

The Messenger smiled, "Very good! Now you need to remember this verse. It can give you peace, strength, help you to forgive others, and help you to understand the unseen spiritual world." The Messenger looked very intensely into the eyes of each of the children. "The Father of Lights has given me a message for all of you, My young friends. Now that you have taken the Oath of Salvation and Life, I know that you are ready to receive the Father's message and guidance. From now on, He will be sending you His love notes and His instructions on life choices very regularly, and as long as you are listening to Him and for Him, He will talk to you more and more. It is called having a relationship with the Father. However, if you don't listen to Him and for Him and follow the instructions and guidance that He sends, He will stop sending them. So you must seek the Father at all times."

The Messenger stood up, and a heavenly light surrounded Him. Everyone's eyes got as big as saucers! He was literally glowing! Then there were crystal clear wings behind Him. They were huge! The children stood there in perfect silence, as if they were frozen. And when He spoke, you could hear the sounds of many rushing waters. "My children, are you ready for the adventures of your destinies to begin? I created you to be victorious in this journey of life. Although the evil one has tried to devour you, now is the time for you to rise up above the obstacles. The roadblocks shall fall before you because I am with you. I am the way, the truth, and the life. A new page has been turned, and a new season is upon you. It is a season without end. Will you step out in faith? Do not fear the unknown. Nothing is unknown to me. I shall show you things to come by My Spirit. Doors are opening ahead of you, and unusual and exciting days are ahead. You shall do exploits in My name. Are you ready to explore new territory? Can you feel the excitement in the atmosphere? Although the world is becoming darker and darker, you are walking into greater glory. My glory is upon you. All of Heaven is rejoicing. The glorious fire that burns within you is the beginning of the evil-busting promised power that you are receiving from your God, the Father of Lights and the Founder of all of creation. Change is upon you. Come, it's time to explore the new territory that I am giving you today. Do not mourn or weep any longer; now is the time of answered prayer. I am your Abba Father who gave My only Son for you. Will I not also give you all things freely with Him? Yes, I will bless you indeed. My mighty right hand is upon you, and evil shall not grieve you. I have granted your request. Because you know Me, you shall be strong and do mighty exploits! Let's go together now;

keep your eyes on Me. You have never been this way before. You are not ordinary but extraordinary. You are warriors for the kingdom of God. You are agents of My secrets. You are in the kingdom's intelligence agency. You are not common but uncommon. You are uniquely qualified by the blood of the lamb. The weapons you fight with are not of this world. You are armed by me and you are dangerous to the kingdom of darkness. Though the world is blind to the things of the spirit, your eyes have been opened. You are my stealth fighters. You are hidden in my son, and you must remember this, the evil is not all knowing, nor all powerful, nor omnipresent. I AM all of those things. He who is in you is far more superior than he who is in the world. Darkness cannot overcome my warriors of light. I have given you the keys to the kingdom of heaven. Whatever you bind on this earth shall be bound in Heaven, and whatever you loose on this earth shall be loosed in Heaven. You were born to take the enemy down. You were born to take the land. You were born into the kingdom to slay giants. You were born for such a time as this. For you walk in the Spirit and not in the flesh. I have given you My Authority and My name. Have no fear, beloved warriors of mine. Awaken to who you are in Me. You are part of the special forces of heaven. The evil one knows that his time is short. I saw him fall like lightening from the heavens. He shall be as nothing to you. I have saved my best and my most powerful fearsome warriors for last. And the gates of the dark underworld shall not prevail against you!" And the Messenger slowly stopped glowing. "Hear the words of the Lord!" He said. By that time, all of the animals in the land had silently gathered around to listen in. The children looked at each other to find that they were all wearing golden armor!

"Wow! I've never seen anything as beautiful as this!" declared Jazelyn.

"Me either!" announced Allan. "We're rich! I can't believe it, we're rich!" he stuttered.

"Hold on a minute," interrupted Michael. "Do we get to keep this golden armor?"

"Of course, you do," said the Messenger. "And it will grow with you. However, no one will be able to see it without spiritual vision."

"That's a bummer!" sighed Derice. "But at least no one can steal it if they can't see it!" All of a sudden, they were standing in Mrs. Joyce's living room.

"What a trip!" said Jazelyn.

"No kidding," said Allan.

"No one's going to believe this," said Michael.

"You're right," said Derice, "so we better keep this information between us for now." Everyone agreed that would be the best option for now. So they hurried to wash their hands and get back to the kitchen where Mrs. Joyce was preparing to make the doggie cookies for the pet shelter.

"I have set up some work stations for you to make your choice of recipes," Mrs. Joyce stated, as she practically floated around her kitchen. "You can make as many as you want until the ingredient supplies run out," she said with a grin and a chuckle. "There are a couple of different recipes to choose from, bake and no bake…" Everyone got right to work and had a ton of fun that wonderful afternoon. It was getting easier for Jazelyn and Allan to work together, and Derice and Michael nearly had a flour fight all in the name of a great time. The hours flew by, and it was time once again to go home. However, they had managed to make what seemed to be a car load of doggie treats.

"Thanks for helping out today, kids," said Mrs. Joyce. "I'll get them delivered first thing tomorrow."

"You are very welcome," announced Jazelyn. "And before I forget, can I talk to you in private before I leave today? Also, is there anything else we can help you with this week?"

"Sure, I'd love to talk to you and answer your questions if I can," Mrs. Joyce smiled. "I hope that all of you can feel comfortable talking to me when you have questions. And as for needing more help, there's always things to do around here. Hmm," sighed Mrs. Joyce. "I was planning on working out in my garden. Does anyone want to help me pull weeds?"

Michael piped up, "Well, actually, I'm pretty good at that," as he leaned over the kitchen countertop.

"We all can do that!" affirmed Allan, overjoyed with the thought of coming back to spend more time with everyone and to find out what else could be waiting for them in The Secrets of the Ages Book. Everyone agreed on a day to do the yardwork, and Mrs. Joyce was very thankful for all the help she could get.

Jazelyn stayed behind while the others went outside in the front yard to size up the chore they had just signed up for. "Mrs. Joyce, I have to ask you about a voice that comes from behind me and gives my special instructions—it's strange and wonderful all at the same time."

"Yes, it certainly is!" Mrs. Joyce perked up. "Now, baby girl, you're speaking my language! I know exactly what you are talking about. And no, you are not crazy. 'You will hear a voice behind you saying, 'This is the way. Follow it whether it turns to the right or the left' (Isa. 30:21). To me, that is one of the most wonderful things about being a keeper of the Word of God. He never leaves us nor forsakes us!" Mrs. Joyce could go on and on about the Lord's grace, mercy, love, you name it—she never gets tired of sharing the Word.

"Thank you so much for answering my question!" exclaimed Jazelyn. "Now I can rest in peace without wondering if I'm really nuts. I have to go now, but I can't wait for next time." She bounced out the door with a new spring in her step, anxious to share Isaiah 30:21 with the others.

Mrs. Joyce glowed almost as bright as The Messenger had. "Thank you, Jazelyn, for making my day! Not only for all the work you kids did for me, but thank you for asking your questions. Truly, that warms my heart more than a warm fire on a cold winter's day! I always look forward to the next time you'll visit." She watched as the kids left her yard, the girls in one direction and the boys in another. Then she said a prayer for each one of them, for the Lord to bless and keep them and protect them as they began their journey as keepers of The Secrets of the Ages Book.

Chapter 5

An Invincible Team

Soon the morning came for everyone to show up at Mrs. Joyce's house for yard detail. The early morning sunlight, soft and diffuse, finally gave way to the first strong, golden rays of the day that bring true warmth. Water evaporated in the gentle breeze to join the white, puffy cloud ships that sailed effortlessly in the ocean of blue sky. Nature sang the ageless song that calls forth a summer's day. Everyone was so excited to get started. Derice, Allan, and Michael all rushed over to Jazelyn's house to help her get her chores finished so that she wouldn't have to be late. More and more, the kids enjoyed spending time together. Savoring each moment is very important. Tomorrow is not guaranteed to anyone. Each playful month will come in moments as a gift of the present.

"We're here to help you with your chores, Jazelyn!" Derice grinned as she flung open the front door, "and I've recruited help too." She continued, "Just show us where to start!"

"That's right," confirmed Allan, ready and willing to grab a broom or a mop.

"What can I do to help?" asked Michael as he bounced through the door.

"Actually," announced Jazelyn, "I just finished. I was just headed out the door to meet you guys."

"Awesome," mumbled Allan, "housework is not my forte." He smiled as he whirled around and extended his hand to Jazelyn like a royal knight in shining armor. For the first time, he noticed her shoulders had an olive glow to them; her skin was flawless. He could scarcely breathe as he watched her every movement. She was everything he wanted, yet she had a way of getting under his skin like no one he had ever met before. Her eyes seemed to have gotten brighter, more brilliant, as they sparkled in the sunlight. She looked like some angel from the celestial heavens. He generally pretended not to notice her, in fear that she wouldn't want to spend time together. But when he did return her glances, he didn't have to try to smile—it just came naturally. Then she would blush ever so slightly in those moments. He knew in his heart that this information must stay hidden for now. He knew that some people are worth the wait, and she is definitely one of them.

Jazelyn grabbed his arm and said, "Come on, Casanova, let's get some weeds pulled before your energy runs out!"

Derice and Michael just laughed and headed out the door.

When they reached Mrs. Joyce's house, she was already out in the yard working.

"Good morning," remarked Mrs. Joyce as she greeted the kids with large straw hats, gardening gloves, and sunscreen spray. "I think we need to have a quick lesson on what weeds look like and what flowers look like," she said with a large grin. "I've had other people help me in the past who ended up pulling more flowers than weeds. So we're not going to go down that road again. It's too much work for me later and too stressing for my flowers to be pulled up and replanted." Mrs. Joyce was a wealth of knowledge. She taught them about medicinal plants and weeds that the pioneers used for healing, being as pharmacies were not on every corner as they are nowadays, and because doctors sometimes were miles away. Life was a lot different then; however, medicinal weeds have their place, but it was not in her prize-winning garden. As they worked, the boys made up jokes and kept the girls entertained until break time.

Mrs. Joyce had filled a large ice chest with bottled water and tons of ice and set up a picnic table under a large shade tree. "Come over here and let's take a break," she called out. Soon, everyone gathered around. "I've also dragged out an inflatable pool I had in the garage and set it up in the backyard," Mrs. Joyce said as she handed out ice-cold water bottles. "I've started filling it with water so that after lunch, it should be filled enough for everyone to get cooled off if you'd like."

"Thank you so much," beamed Jazelyn.

Everyone chimed in, "Yes, thank you, Mrs. Joyce."

"Awesome," declared Michael. "Allan, I'm going to baptize you this afternoon!"

"What does that mean?" demanded Allan. All he could think about was the time that his brother's friends held him upside down and flushed his head in the toilet.

Mrs. Joyce noticed quickly Allan's uneasy look on his face. "Do any of you know what baptism is?" She could see an oncoming war between the boys. She knew that the truth sets people free, so it was definitely time for some truth. "Does anyone know why it's important for Christians to do it?"

"Baptism is a symbol of Jesus's death and resurrection, like in the Easter story," said Jazelyn.

"That's right," said Mrs. Joyce. "Romans 6:4-5 says, 'We were therefore buried with him (Jesus) through baptism into death in order that, just as Christ was raised from the dead through the glory of the Father, we too may live a new life.' Jesus is our example," Mrs. Joyce continued. "Jesus was baptized" in Matthew 3:13-17: 'Then Jesus came from Galilee to the Jordan to be baptized by John. But John tried to deter him, saying, 'I need to be baptized by you, and do you come to me?' Jesus replied, 'Let it be so for now; it is proper for us to do this to fulfill all righteousness.' Then John consented. As soon as Jesus was baptized, he went up out of the water. At that moment heaven was opened, and he saw the Spirit of God descending like a dove and alighting on him. And a voice from heaven said, 'This is my son, in whom I love; with him I am well pleased.'" Mrs. Joyce still continued, "Baptism is a symbol; repentance comes before baptism. Baptism is a symbol of the death of our sin and our new life beginning with Christ. Acts 2:38, 'Peter replied, 'Repent and be baptized, every one of you, in the name of Jesus Christ for the forgiveness of your sins. And you will receive the gift of the Holy Spirit.' And Acts 8:35-36, 38-39 says, 'Then Phillip began with that very passage of Scripture and told him the good news about Jesus. As they traveled along the road, they came to some water and the eunuch said, 'Look, here is water. What can stand in the way of my being baptized?'...And he gave orders to stop the chariot. Then both Phillip and the eunuch went down into the water and Phillip baptized him. When they came up out of the water, the Spirit of the Lord suddenly took Phillip away, and the eunuch did not see him again, but went on his way rejoicing.' Baptism is about identification," continued Mrs. Joyce. "When a believer is baptized, he or she publicly identifies with Jesus and other Christians. To identify with someone is to say that you are with that person—that you belong together, like in a family or a group." She said, "Baptism is a symbol. It's a physical picture of a spiritual reality. When you see someone being baptized, you're watching a moving picture of what has happened to that person spiritually. Baptism is also a picture of our death. The person being baptized goes under the water, which is a picture of the burial of his or her old self that was enslaved to sin. We are as dead to our sin as Jesus was dead on the cross. Jesus really died on the cross, and they buried Him. When we put our trust in Jesus Christ to save us, God's Word assures us that we really died to our sin and our old selves were buried along with Jesus. Baptism is a picture of our resurrection. The person being baptized is brought up out of the water, which is a picture of his or her soul being raised from the dead to eternal life. Being brought up out of the water is also a forward-looking picture. It reminds us of God's promise to one day resurrect our physical bodies from the grave, just like He did for Jesus." Mrs. Joyce intently watched everyone's reactions, "Does anyone have any questions?"

"Sure," said Allan. "When can we get baptized?"

"I'm already baptized," said Jazelyn. "I was baptized a couple of years ago at our church picnic in the park down by the river."

"I was baptized about a year ago," said Michael. "My grandpa baptized me down at the river, and he told me that now I could baptize others as long, as they except Jesus as their Lord and Savior. Grandpa says there's no Jr. Holy Spirit."

"Well, I want to be baptized too," said Derice. "I've wanted to for a long time, ever since Jazelyn got baptized, but I didn't know who to talk to about it."

"Why didn't you ask me?" asked Jazelyn. "We could have talked to my dad."

"I guess I felt like your dad wouldn't want to talk to me about it," moaned Derice.

"Nonsense, we can talk to him tonight," said Jazelyn.

"We'll talk more about it after a while," exclaimed Mrs. Joyce. "Why don't you kids finish pulling those weeds on the side of the house, and I'll go make up some sandwiches for lunch. What are your favorite kinds?" she asked as she headed for the back porch.

"Peanut butter and jelly or turkey or tuna are my favorites," said Allan, "but I'll eat almost anything."

"Sounds good to me," said Michael. "I like those choices too."

"Turkey or tuna for me, please," said Derice.

"I like peanut butter without jelly for me," said Jazelyn. "Do you want me to help you, Mrs. Joyce?"

"No thanks, sweetie," answered Mrs. Joyce. "These days, it's easier for me to make sandwiches than pull weeds. I'll call you kids when it's time to wash up." Everyone hurried to get back to work. They all were anxious to get finished so they could enjoy the blow-up pool that was filling with water in the back yard. They anticipated a great afternoon in the cool paddling pool; even though they all wished the pool was a lot bigger, any water puddle was welcome on a hot, sunny, sweltering day.

By a quarter after twelve noon, Mrs. Joyce stepped out on the back porch and announced, "Lunch time! Everyone pick up your weeds and put them in the compost pile. Clean up and bring all your hats, gloves, and water bottles up to the porch, and go wash up for lunch—and don't forget to use warm water and lots of soap!" The kids could not wait to get into the living room and open The Secrets of the Ages Book. What awaited in those pages today? Where would they go? What would they see? It was a race to see who could get into the house first. It was a neck-to-neck finish between the girls and the boys. As they bounced through the back door, they could see that Mrs. Joyce had prepared a smorgasbord of sandwich choices, complete with lemonade and cookies. The smells that wafted from Mrs. Joyce's kitchen were absolutely heavenly. Nevertheless, The Secrets of the Ages Book was beckoning them. Down the hallway they dashed, darted into the living room, and stood before the large, beautifully bound book. Their hearts were pounding. With a sigh and a deep breath, Allan slowly and carefully opened the cover. The pages started flipping themselves, and in a flash, the living room was gone and the children were standing in a beautiful garden. Within a twinkling of an eye, the Messenger was standing behind them.

"Welcome, My young friends, I've been waiting for you," He gently whispered with His deep, soft, loving voice. "Today is a very special day," He announced. "Today you will witness the most wonder things!" He turned and pointed north. "We'll be traveling this way—please follow me." Without hesitation, they quickly followed the Messenger. They walked down a cobblestone path that wound down through an emerald green garden with tall trees and a rainbow of flowers with the brightest colors anyone had ever seen before splattered in delicate clusters along the edges of the stony path. The fragrances were amazing; dewdrops covered the leaves of each plant that brought a coolness in the air that was most welcome on that sticky summer's day.

"What are we going to see today?" inquired Allan.

"You'll find out soon enough," The Messenger replied. Just then, everyone heard the voice behind them saying,

"I am He who is called Faithful and True. I am your Fierce Protector. I understand what you face and go through every day. I am the Author and Finisher of your faith. Depend on My faith when you cannot find your own. I am Immanuel, God with you. I will never leave you, nor forsake you. I will not fail you. I am your strength, and I have given you a measure of My faith. Cling to Me; lean on Me. I am your hope of glory. I have made you an overcomer. Although you have tribulations in this world, be of good cheer for I have overcome the world."

"Thank you, Mr. Messenger for all the time you spent with us and for everything you teach us," commented Jazelyn.

"You are more than welcome, and being thankful is one of the most important things you can be," answered the Messenger. "Be sure you never forget that. The Father says, 'I hear your deepest sighs and groanings, and they touch My heart deeply. They are your wordless prayers—yes, perfect prayers prayed by My Holy Spirit. I am well-acquainted with your griefs and sorrows. My Holy Spirit is in you travailing and interceding for you. I know that you do not always have the words to say when you are hurting and in distress. But My Comforter has come to abide inside you to help you. Inside your heart resides truth and wisdom, so do not be anxious about anything. Lay down your heavy burdens at My feet and rest in My perfect love."

Soon, they crested a small hill. There they were able to see the River of Destiny, and over it was a huge crystal bridge. There were angels rushing back and forth over the magnificent bridge. They were carrying prayers over the bridge and bringing blessing back to where they came from. There were a massive number of angels coming and going, each one dressed in the whitest of white garments.

"What is on the other side?" gasped Jazelyn. "I've never seen such a wonderful place!"

"This place is totally amazing!" sighed Derice.

The Messenger gazed over to the land across the beautiful bridge. He suddenly seemed to be taller than before, and if you looked close, you could almost see huge wings behind Him that were as clear as glass. "That, my young friends, is the place of the throne room of the Father. He sits on His throne and appears like the crystalline sparkle of a jasper stone and the fiery redness of a sardius stone, and encircling the throne is a rainbow that looks like the color of an emerald. And surrounding His throne are twenty-four other thrones; and there are twenty-four elders dressed in white clothing with crowns of gold on their heads. From the Father's throne come flashes of lightning and rumbling sounds and thunder. Seven lamps of fire burn in front of His throne, which are the seven Spirits of God the Father. And in front of the throne is like a sea of glass, like the clearest crystal. In the center and around the throne are four living creatures who are full of eyes in front and behind, seeing everything and knowing everything that is around them. The first living creature is like a lion. The second creature like an ox, the third creature has the face of a man, and the fourth creature is like a flying eagle. And the four living creatures, each one of them having six wings, day and night they never stop saying, 'Holy, Holy, Holy is the Lord God, the Almighty—who was and who is and who is to come.' He is the Omnipotent, the Ruler of all, the unchanging, eternal God. Whenever the living creatures give glory and honor and thanksgiving to Him who sits on the throne, to

Him who lives forever and ever, the twenty-four elders fall down before Him who sits on the throne, and they worship Him who lives forever and ever; and they throw down their crowns before the throne, saying, 'Worthy are You, our Lord and God, to receive the glory and the honor and the power; for You created all things, and because of Your will, they exist and were created and brought into being.'"

Down along the riverbank below the bridge was a long beach where angels waited for assignments. "Listen," said the Messenger, "hear the heartbeat of the River of Life flowing from the Throne of Grace. There is a wonderful breaking free of the bondages of this earth. It is the glorious rhythm of a rushing river, refusing to be held back by the strongholds that the enemy has attempted to build up against the children of the Father of Lights." The Messenger looked at the children. "Are you ready for another message from your Father the Creator and Keeper of all things?"

"Yes, Sir," piped up Michael, "I love getting messages from the Father."

"We all do!" chimed in Derice, soaking in every sight, sound, and fragrance she was experiencing.

The Messenger started to glow again. "I have given My angels charge over you," says the Father of Lights. "They are encamped all around you. They hearken to the voice of My Word. I have given you the authority to speak My Word. When you speak My Word, it is the same as if I was speaking it. Do not feel that you are unworthy of this blessing by the blood of the Lamb; I have pardoned all your iniquities and redeemed your lives from the pit. I have crowned you with lovingkindness and compassion. I want you to speak forth My Word and My name to give your angels something they can work with. This is a benefit afforded only to those who are born-again by My Spirit. Do not give a voice to your fears. Diligently listen for My Voice in your mouth. Without fail, My angels who are mighty in strength and who are given an exceeding might of intellect, force, and voice that they delight in using in sacred services for you will hear you speak My words and respond. The things that are impossible for man are possible with your God. I have sent My heavenly warriors to do My pleasure, and they are always ready to hear and know and follow explicitly My declared and decreed will that comes from your lips. Fear not, My angels are encamped around you to guard and rescue you. Even now, you entertain angels unaware."

In a blink, the kids were back in Mrs. Joyce's living room.

"Wow, that's so awesome!" said Derice. "I love our trips into The Secrets of the Ages Book!"

"Me too!" agreed Michael. "But we better get washed up with warm water and soap and get back to the kitchen before Mrs. Joyce comes looking for us." Everyone laughed and agreed. They got back to the kitchen to find Mrs. Joyce talking with the pastor of her church.

"Come on in, kids, I want you to meet our pastor." She was pouring everyone a glass of lemonade. "Can you stay for sandwiches and lemonade, Pastor Greg?"

"Sure, I would love to meet your gardeners," he said with a large grin. "I was just walking by and couldn't help but notice the excellent job you kids are doing."

Michael thought about all the good things his grandparents had told him about the pastor, and for the first time, he finally made since of it. He could hear them in his memories. "Everything about the pastor was a soft understated joy as he greeted each person. Some people wear a smile, but he was the smile. The members of his congregation were the patients in his surgery. Their lives welcomed the emotions that tumbled out of his sermons. How many people have gone on to be better friends, better bosses, better parents from the spreading out of the goodness of just one man and his lovely wife. When your world explodes from the inside, he is the man you want standing next to you. He feels the shockwave and stays on his feet. Whatever he had to do disappears as he refocuses on what needs to be done. He will cover every angle and stay right there until you can breathe again, walk and talk at the same time again. Then he stands back and lets you get on with your world, never mentioning your crisis again." Michael smiled as he listened to the pastor talking about how he wished his own children had a passion for gardening.

"I was raised on a small farm and enjoyed the fruits of a large garden when I was a kid." The pastor seemed to relax as he shared the memories of his childhood with the others. After lunch, they sat out on the back porch and talked about all the wonderful things that Mrs. Joyce had taught them over the summer. The pastor smiled from ear to ear. "Mrs. Joyce will never retire as long as there are people willing to learn the truths that she teaches."

"That's right!" sighed Mrs. Joyce "My work is cut out for me!"

The pastor leaned forward and whispered to the kids, "Do you want to know what the most important thing I've ever learned is?" There was complete silence in the room.

"Yes!" whispered Jazelyn.

"I do too," whispered Allan.

"That goes for us too!" quietly nodded Derice and Michael.

"Many people cannot understand or comprehend the importance of what I'm about to share with you. Nevertheless, since you are in training to be keepers of the Secrets of the Ages. I know that you will need to know this very important information." The pastor paused a moment.

"It's to be quick to repent!—to tell the Lord you're sorry when you mess up and do not do it again, to understand that you are heading in the wrong direction and it's unprofitable, so you turn and go in another direction.

In Mark 1:15 it says, 'The time has come, the kingdom of God has come near. Repent and believe the good news!' Also, Psalm 32:2 is a wonderful place to learn about the nature and process of true repentance. 'How happy is the man the Lord does not charge with sin, and in whose spirit is no deceit!' Be honest about your need for repentance. Everyone has done something that is unpleasing to our Father God. Repentance requires honesty. We must first acknowledge our need for forgiveness and reconciliation with the Lord.

Only those who have stopped trying to cover up their sin with self-righteousness and deceit can experience the deep and lasting change that only comes though repentance. In addition, we need to acknowledge the danger of sin and the damage that guilt can cause. 'When I kept silent, my bones became brittle from my groaning all day long. For day and night, your hand was heavy on me; my strength was drained as in the summer's heat' (Ps. 32:3-4). We seek repentance because God's spirit has convicted us. Sometimes we often blame others for our stress and general moodiness, but many times we simply feel bad because we've done bad things. David describes physical and emotional symptoms associated with a guilty conscience. Honestly, we must address the consequences of our sin, which means assessing both personal consequences and the impact they have had and will continue to have on others. And confess fully. Deep repentance calls for full confession. The only way to be truly sure that we are covered by Christ is to fully expose your sin. We fight to be utterly transparent before God about the depth and breadth of our sin. Ruthless honesty will bring forth freedom and joy. Then, hide in God. 'You took away the guilt of my sin. Therefore, let everyone who is faithful pray to you at a time when you may be found. When the great floodwaters come, they will not reach him. You are my hiding place; You protect me from trouble. You surround me with joyful shouts of deliverance' (Ps. 32:5b-7). Adam and Eve hid behind self-made coverings to mask their sin and shame. We too often hide behind self-made righteousness in order to make ourselves appear more acceptable than we really are. If you want to change, to really change—which, by the way, is the mark of true repentance—then you must hide in God alone."

Allan got a strange look on his face. "Does that mean you kind of go into a witness protection program?"

"Yes, I think it would be a lot like that—you move, you change, and you begin a new life and don't go back to the old ways." The pastor smiled. He could see that his words were not wasted. These kids were honestly, seriously, interested in learning about God's ways. "Then you seize the hope. 'Many pains come to the wicked, but the one who trusts in the LORD will have faithful love surrounding him' (Ps. 32:11). How can you be sure God will forgive you?—by His unfailing love. Surely you can find reassurance in the great promises He has made throughout history, and how they have been fulfilled in Jesus Christ:

His promise to Adam and Eve to crush the enemy.

His promise to Abraham to claim and protect a people.

His promise to David to provide a once-and-for-all eternal King for His people.

All throughout history God has been saying and continues to tell us, 'I love you; I will not fail you; I am enough.' Look to the promises of God, seize the hope, and 'be glad in the LORD and rejoice, you righteous ones; shout for joy, all you upright in heart!' (Ps. 32:11). Always remember that 1 Samuel 17:47 tells us that the battle belongs to the Lord.

Evil has a battle plan. It wants to take your focus off of the truth and put it on what you see and experience instead."

"Thanks for sharing that with us!" said Allan. "And while you're here, I have another question. It's about baptism."

The pastor's eyes twinkled as he smiled. He praised God in his heart for another soul was about to enter the kingdom of God! All of heaven was rejoicing! "That is a great question!" replied the pastor. "In the New Testament, baptism came almost immediately after a person's profession of faith. (Paul spelled it out in Rom. 6:3 and 1 Cor. 6). It should be a clear, simple, uncomplicated, grasp of the gospel, which is what baptism symbolically depicts. A person must understand that they are a sinner. The first question we ask is, 'Do you repent of your sins and acknowledge your need of a Savior?' In following Jesus, we must acknowledge our need for Him and that we are repenting and turning away from sin. Paul puts it this way: 'Do you not know that all of us who have been baptized into Christ Jesus were baptized into his death? (Rom. 6:3). It is not the act of baptism itself that buries our old, sinful nature, but rather, baptism is a symbol of us going to the grave with Jesus. 'We were buried therefore with him by baptism into death" (Rom. 6:4). Isn't that beautiful? Our brokenness, our shame, our sin, our guilt, are put in the grave. We are turning from our old sinful nature when we repent and turn to Jesus. The second question is: 'Have you put your faith in Jesus as your Lord and Savior?' It is not enough to turn from sin; it's about turning to Jesus as the only one who can save. Saying that we have put our faith in Him means we believe in our hearts and acknowledge with our mouths that Jesus is God in the flesh, that He conquered over death, and that He alone has the power to save. And because of our faith in Jesus, we are raised, just as

He was raised to new life! Just as Christ was raised from the dead by the glory of the Father, we too might walk in newness of life. 'For if we have been united with Him in a death like His, we shall certainly be united with Him in a resurrection like His' (Rom. 6:4). This is why we cheer, shout, clap, jump, and celebrate for those who are being baptized as they emerge from the water because it's a picture of their new life found in Jesus. They have been raised from their spiritual death and now are able to live by the life-giving Spirit of Jesus. Therefore, here is what we say to someone just before they enter into the waters in this beautiful symbol of redemption. 'Because of your repentance of sin and faith in Jesus, today we acknowledge your old self is buried with Christ and you have been to new life in Jesus! Therefore, I baptize you in the name of the Father, the Son, and the Holy Spirit!'

There is nothing special about the water, but there is something so deep and meaningful about what it symbolizes. The water symbolizes our grave, where we go to die. So when we raise from that grave, we raise more alive than ever before."

"Thanks again!" said Allan. "I know for sure now that I'm getting baptized!"

The pastor gave Allan a thumbs up. "Just let me know when and where you want to be baptized, and I'll be there!"

Allan grinned ear to ear. "Awesome! Meet me in the backyard in a little while!"

"Has anyone checked on the blow-up pool lately?" asked Allan. "It's probably full enough to get into by now."

"Great!" yelled Michael as he ran to check the pool's filling progress. "Hey, Allan, do you want me to baptize you?"

"Yes, I do!" giggled Allan as he ran after Michael. For the first time, Allan felt his atmosphere change. His youthful exuberance exploded into leadership that day. He knew in his heart that from this day forward, everything would be different than before. He would stand taller, breathe deeper, because he had found what so many people had searched for their entire lives—his own personal relationship with the King of Kings and Lord of Lords, the Father of Lights.

"Me too!" yelled Derice right behind the boys, anxious to feel the cool water rushing through her fingers as ribbons of silk. There was a thankfulness in her heart. She finally felt that she belonged, not only with her friends but in the family of God.

And so, it was a great day to be baptized! With Pastor Greg standing by, Michael baptized Allan and Derice, and all of heaven rejoiced!

Chapter 6

The Battle for the Living Dead

A few days later, Mrs. Joyce met the girls at the corner market. "It is so nice to see you girls. I was going to visit you this afternoon to see if you and the boys would like to come over and help out decorating and serving some of my friends the day after tomorrow?"

"Are you having a party?" asked Derice.

"Well, kind of," Mrs. Joyce slightly turned away as a large crocodile tear rolled down her face. "One of my dearest friends has passed away, so I'm having a celebration of life for her family and friends. We'll need to set up a memory board and pick a bunch of flowers to put in vases and display around my home."

"Of course, we will!" stated Jazelyn, almost ready to cry herself. "We will tell Allan and Michael. I'm pretty sure they will want to help out also."

"That's for sure!" commented Derice. "Allan never turns down an opportunity to hang out with Jazlyn!" Also it would be a prime opportunity to visit The Secrets of the Ages Book again. It was too good to pass up! "That book is simply amazing!" she thought to herself. Everyone agreed to come help set up and serve punch, lemonade, delicate hors d'oeuvres and finger sandwiches for the grieving family and friends. Soon the day had arrived. The kids were early to Mrs. Joyce's home.

"Welcome, my young friends! Thank you so much for helping out!" Mrs. Joyce met them at the front door. "Let's gather flowers and leave the stems as long as possible," she smiled as she handed everyone snippers. "As soon as we get set up, we should have time to relax a bit before the service at the gravesite starts. Would you like to stay here and greet people as they show up?"

"Yes, please, we wouldn't want to make anyone wait to come in and enjoy what we have prepared for them." Jazlyn tried to comfort Mrs. Joyce as she watched her holding back the tears. Grief kept rolling in like waves on the shore, engulfing and overwhelming her elderly friend. With her spiritual eyes, she could see the darkness unfolding like a cloak of sadness, while a multitude of unforgettable memories flooded over her mind and leaked out her swollen eyes as proof of an enduring love shared between the dearest of friends. "Are you okay Mrs. Joyce?" asked Jazelyn as she tucked her arm around her.

"Yes, dear, these are just tears of sadness and joy. I will dearly miss her, but I know she is with Jesus now and not in pain any longer. My friend was blessed beyond measure because she knew Jesus as her Lord and Savior. She always had a hope for the future that many people do not have because they do not know the Lord. Every day here on earth, we walk through a valley of lost souls, usually never knowing and most of the time, not caring. So many people live their lives entangled in sin, thinking that they will repent and tell the Lord sorry right before their lives are over. However, we are only one breath away from eternity. Everything changes in a blink of an eye. Please promise me you won't forget to share the Bible and its wonders with others."

"We won't forget—we promise," said Allan.

"Thank you, Mrs. Joyce, for taking the time to teach us!" piped up Michael.

"Yes, thank you, I will always think of you as the grandma I never had," chimed in Derice.

"You know I won't forget to share the Bible!" smiled Jazelyn.

A sigh of relief came over Mrs. Joyce. "I am so blessed to have you all as friends. I'm very thankful and most grateful for all of you. Now we better hurry and get the house ready. I need to leave soon." Everyone pitched in, and everything came together quickly, and soon, Mrs. Joyce was out the door and on her way to the service. They all stood at the door and waved as she drove out of sight.

"Well, I guess we better visit The Secrets of the Ages Book— this might be the last time for a while since school will be starting soon, and who knows when we can be able to do this again," Allan sighed, staring at walls that had become so familiar over the summer. He would always remember the soft tinkling of the wind chimes and the summer afternoons spent out on Mrs. Joyce's porch with his new best friends.

"I'm really going to miss hanging out here!" said Michael. "If anything happened to Mrs. Joyce, I'm sure I'd cry like it was my own grandma." His fondest memories were being in the garden. He loved the misty blue hydrangeas that reminded him of his grandfather who had the greenest thumb in the world, according to himself. And, of course, the adventures inside The Secrets of the Ages Book! Absolutely nothing could ever top that.

"Me too," murmured Derice. "She's been so good to us, and I really didn't treat her very nicely when I first met her." Her heart was heavy with sorrow; sorry seemed so meaningless and overused. Saying sorry doesn't fix the hurt you have caused someone—"sorry" is just a word. It's when you truly mean it in your heart that it becomes powerful enough to move mountains.

As the kids slowly made their way down the long hallway to visit the book, the voice from behind spoke as clear as day.

"You are the secret weapons of My kingdom. You are dunamis firepower of the Father's arsenal—the walking epistles, My gentle ones who are as wise as the serpent but as gentle as the dove. Your prayers and worship are the warfare that happens before the enemy is aware of your presence. The victory is won before the battle even begins.

I have declared, 'It is finished.' Do you understand how your praise and worship has become a mighty weapon? It is a fire burning in your heart that is released by the Holy Spirit. The enemy cannot see where you are coming from or where you are going. The evil will never know what hit it as you move in the leading of the Holy Spirit. Fear not, My children. You are more than conquerors through Him who loves you. Every place your feet treads shall become holy ground unto the Lord. This is how you will fight your battles—you shall ambush the enemy with your praise and worship, and you shall watch the enemy fall. The God of peace will soon crush Satan the slanderer under your feet.

I am your Deliverer. Whatever situation you find yourself in, call upon Me. I will deliver you from the ravenous evil beasts who threaten to consume you. There is nothing that can happen to you that I will not make a way of escape for you. I am the same yesterday, today, tomorrow, and forever. Let your faith speak louder than your fear. I have already won the victory. I have heard your cries, and I shall deliver you out of all your troubles."

The very moment they opened The Secrets of the Ages Book, they were standing right in front of the Forest of Lost Souls. It was dark and damp with an eerie chill in the air. Allan gasped, "I never expected this!"

"Look at us!" said Michael. "We've got our golden armor on!" There they stood with gleaming swords of fire and armor forged from the finest gold. The group was encircled by a mighty host of angelic beings, everyone having flaming swords and golden armor.

You could hear the whimpers and cries of the lost souls, "Help us; please save us." Evil was lurking everywhere. Dark shadows were flying over their heads and crouching, ready to pounce like a hoard of hungry lions and ravenous wolves. Michael and Allan with their angelic guards were on point. Jazelyn and Derice with their angels were the rear guards. There were dark, raggedy skeleton soldiers that were guarding the entrance of the bridge that lead into the Forest of Lost Souls.

The battle began. The angels of light ran at the dark soldiers with their blazing swords and slashed them into pieces. However, the dingy, raggedy bones kept flying back together, and the battle continued until an army of other heavenly creatures flew in and carried the bones to the far corners of the earth, preventing them from ever reconnecting again. They battled until all of the darkness in their path was destroyed.

As they walked deeper into the dark forest, a pungent order began to get stronger and stronger until the stench of rottenness filled the air like pea soup.

"What on earth is that terrible smell?" asked Jazelyn. "That definitely has to be the worst thing I've ever smelled!" she said as she rummaged through her pocket for a tissue to use as a breathing mask.

At once, The Messenger was standing right there beside them. "That is the stench of sin," He said. "Do you remember what the Father told you today?" Michael immediately started speaking the Word of God, declaring and decreeing the Father's promises. Everyone else followed suit.

The group began to radiate a warm glow. As they spoke the scriptures louder and louder, the glory fell from heaven, and the glow became brighter and brighter! "Holy, Holy, Holy is the Lord God Almighty!" became their chant. The darkness was powerless against it.

Again, the voice from behind spoke: "Although you may feel surrounded by the enemy, it is only a smokescreen. It is a trick of the enemy to get you to take your eyes off of your Heavenly Father. In reality, I have surrounded you with angel armies and My favor, like a shield. You are surrounded by My goodness, My glory and My everlasting arms. What I have given you is no ordinary goodness nor is it comparable to the glory of any man. It is supernatural, above and beyond what you have ever seen or dared to imagine. It is beyond any man's comprehension when you see it and know it by the Spirit. I am able to do exceedingly abundantly above all that you ask or think, according to the power that works in you. Fear not for I am with you always, even to the ends of the world."

Soon they came upon a small clearing where some cages were strewn about in a haphazard manner, as if naughty children had thrown down their toys to turn their attentions elsewhere. Jazelyn noticed something moving in the cages, something oddly familiar or someone oddly familiar. There were the sounds of sobbing coming from those cages.

"Who are you?" asked Derice.

"Don't you know? You see me at school all the time but never talk to me," said the small weary voice from the cage. "Don't stay here. Leave now before you end up like us, captured and caged like animals with no hope of escaping."

"I do know you! You've been in some of my classes. You are the quiet girl," said Derice. "We will not leave without you!" Derice swung her flaming sword, and the door of the cage flung open. A small frail shadow crawled out of the cage.

"I am one of the living dead. My humanly body is at my home in the city, but I have nothing to live for, so the evil darkness has kept my mind imprisoned here," the shadow said as she stood there feeling empty and lost.

"Who wants to go home and learn about the Father of Lights and The Secrets of the Ages Book—The Basic Instructions Before Leaving Earth?" asked Jazelyn. "Each one of you has an incredible destiny that the Father of Lights has prepared for you from the foundations of the world!" All of the caged shadows started shaking their cages and begging not to be left behind. "Open the cages, boys!" yelled Jazelyn.

"And everyone who wants to fulfil the destiny that you were created for, stay inside our circle of Holy Spirit fire, and let's go home!"

All the way home they chanted, "We will win the battles with our worship, prayers, and the word of our testimonies!" Their mission had become more real than ever—to save people, to tell the world about the promises of our Heavenly Father! There were still dark shadows lurking and hovering in the misty woods; however, none would dare come close to the bright glow that was created when the kids worshipped the Father. The darkness slithered and shrunk away hiding from the light. Before you know it, everyone was right back in Mrs. Joyce's living room.

"Let's get washed up and be ready for everyone when they get here. It shouldn't be long now," Jazelyn said as she noticed her skin was still glowing. In fact, they all were still glowing.

The Messenger smiled, "That's what happens when you spend time in the presence of God, and sometimes, you have gold dust that sticks to you!" He tipped his hat and vanished once again. Then the voice from behind said, "I will never leave you nor forsake you. Fear not!"

Just then, there was a knock on the door. They rushed to greet and serve everyone at the celebration of life that Mrs. Joyce had prepared with such loving care.

Just as it always happens, summer had lightened its grasp; mornings had the chill of fall. The hands of the clock stop for no one. It was time for Jazelyn, Derice, Allan, and Michael to start another year of high school. That summer had forged an unbreakable bond between the four, the kind of friendship that will last a lifetime. Jazelyn vowed to herself to make the future as brilliant as she had dreamed it could be, to search and find the joy and wonder in the small things in life, and to share the magnificent Secrets of the Ages with anyone who would be willing to listen. She continued to hear the voice from behind and followed its guidance and instruction, which kept her safe many times and led her to many divine appointments over the years to come. They all joined the youth group at Pastor Greg's church, which, by the way, grew into hundreds over the next few years. Michael became a youth leader that year and began helping Pastor Greg with the baptisms. He and Allan recruited most of the gang members into youth group, including Allan's brother, and by the end of the following summer, most of them were baptized and had changed lives also.

The coolness brought the scents of cinnamon, apple, and pumpkin spice wafting all over town. Soon a chill would creep into the air that would start the cycle of colorful canopies of red, scarlet, golden yellows, and various shades of brown leaves. It would be time to get ready to let go and allow the restful sleep of a winter's nap to continue the cycle of life.

Everyone started back to school, and, for now, the story is only just beginning. This summer had awakened the holy, supernatural reality of destiny in the four young people. The memories of the summer became cherished stories that would be repeated and would be celebrated in the heavenly realms throughout all eternity.

The End

CPSIA information can be obtained
at www.ICGtesting.com
Printed in the USA
LVHW071502070422
715625LV00007B/188